Hawkes In Flight

by

Claude M. Higgins, Jr.

First published by AuthorHouse 06/12/04

ISBN: 1-4184-5471-0 (e-book)
ISBN: 1-4184-5472-9 (Paperback)

Library of Congress Control Number: 2004105060

This book is printed on acid free paper.

Printed in the United States of America
Bloomington, IN

To the Reader: This book is a compilation of memories written by Claude M. Higgins, Jr. As he wrote his memories, he changed the names of people and places. He also used his imagination to embellish or to enhance many of the incidents; thus it is autobiographical fiction. The stories are roughly in chronological order. The reader may wish to choose in which order to read the stories. The collection as a whole describes the life of a remarkable man.

TABLE OF CONTENTS

PART FOUR

MEMORIES OF FAMILY AND FRIENDS..................275

PROLOGUE - **MYRON THE SHRINK**

With great reluctance, I began seeing a psychiatrist in the early eighties. I was forty-five, had taught in the public schools for about a quarter of a century, had been suffering a variety of digestive ailments, and was greatly depressed from suffering through many family illnesses and deaths, and many years of stress in the classroom. My personal physician, Dr. Bob Mc Gregor, friend and fellow social activist, had told me that I was not quite right, and should see his friend, Dr. Myron Finestein, MD. and shrink extraordinary.

Naturally, macho Rock's first reaction was that this was a ridiculous suggestion. Everyone knew about head-shrinkers. I certainly didn't need a psychiatrist, but I went anyway. It was an extremely lucky capitulation on my part.

The first meeting was certainly not what I expected. I climbed two flights of stairs and knocked on a door in an old Victorian brick building which had been restored on Windy Gap's newly built hippie mall. A voice from within said, "I'll be out in a minute.' After a few minutes a bushy-haired, smallish Jewish man came into the small waiting room and led me into a dark corner office. There was a desk, a bookshelf, one chair, and a dozen cushions pushed against two walls of the room. The shrink said, "Call me Myron, Rock."

Then he went into a dark corner and flopped down on one of the cushions.

"Sit in the chair if you would be more comfortable there,' he said. The voice from the dark corner asked me to tell him exactly how I felt, physically and mentally. For the next fifteen minutes, I slowly ran through a litany of complaints without any answering comment from Myron. Finally I shut up, and we sat there in the darkness for five minutes.

Then he said, "Rock, I think that you are more than a little crazy." My reaction to this pronouncement was an immediate feeling of anger, and since I had always been an aggressive cowboy type, I replied, "You're full of shit."

Thus began a three year progression through the confusion and anger in my mind. Once a week for more than a year, and then irregularly after that, Myron and I waged our war in his small dark office. During this first year, it was never easy to climb the stairs to his office, and during the beginning weeks, I left at the end of our hour, more often than not, even more angry and increasingly sad about what our conversations had revealed to me.

After about two months of this torture, I decided to turn the tables on him, and I began to probe into Myron's words and behavior. For a while it was hard to tell who was the shrink, and who was the sicko. The interesting thing was that the more I probed, the more sympathy and compassion I had for him, and for myself, and the more I learned about him, the more I learned to like and respect this strange little man. He had been a labor organizer in New York before he went to medical school, and we shared a similar perception of the political process. He was recently divorced. His son had been a student in my wife's elementary school classroom, so I had her perception of him as a starting point. His divorce had shattered him, and, like me, he appeared to be looking for validation of self, and perhaps, a new identity.

Myron suggested that I bring my wife, Summer, to a few of our sessions. These meetings turned into a verbal tennis match between my sweet Summer and her unbalanced husband. Myron watched and listened quietly without injecting much comment of his own. He was letting us swab our own decks. Finally, he met privately with Summer for a few hours, and then suggested that she continue psychoanalysis with a female colleague of his. Summer was to meet with this lady for about a year after that. We were both now delving into the maelstrom of our past and present.

After about a year of seeing Myron on a weekly basis, I began to understand what he was trying to do with me, and I was finally aware of the direction that he felt I should progress toward. Climbing the stairs to his office was no longer such a difficult task. I felt that I was getting better, and that Myron had literally saved my marriage, and to some extent, he had saved my life as well, as I had been suicidal.

I think that the real breakthrough came when Myron and I sat one day discussing an episode of "M*A*S*H" that both of us had watched on television the preceding week. In that particular episode Hawkeye Pierce had found himself on a busload of Korean citizens who were suffering the traumas of the war which had overwhelmed their country. The hero of this piece didn't know how he got there, or why he felt such a great personal pain and confusion in the midst of the agony of these war victims. He mistook the crying of a baby for that of a squawking chicken, and when he shouted at the woman to keep the child quiet, she smothered the baby. In the TV story, Hawkeye finally got off the bus, realizing his guilt and pain, but now at least, off the bus.

Myron said, "You are on your own bus, Rock. The only way to get off is to open the door and step out. Then you have to stand back and try to be sensitive as to what is happening to those folks, and how a change in your thinking and behavior might make all of them, and you, yourself, better able to handle the conditions in which all of us find ourselves."

This simple explanation of the necessity to accept reality, and of the fact that I could make something better for all by my acceptance of things as they were, and by my admission to myself that I was 'on the bus" and needed to get off, suddenly made our years of conversation take on a clear and definite meaning. Myron had been instrumental in my finding, once again, the path which was to lead to acceptance, and ultimately, happiness. But we still had a long way to go.

PART ONE
BACKGROUND AND BOYHOOD

Claude M. Higgins, Jr.

INTRODUCTION TO PART ONE

The Hawke family prayer has gone on for at least six generations : "God, if only I had a chance to relive the past, I would do so many things differently. However, since the past is unchangeable, the only thing that I can do is to live in the present and move on."

Ain't it strange what a little perspective will do for your mind? For fifty years I was so involved in the struggle to survive that I didn't really think much about what was happening around me, what my country really looked like, or who the resident inhabitants of my region were. I had a somewhat deprived childhood, but in many ways it was also fortuitous My name is Rock Hawke. My own people are a very old people, and my land is a very old land. I feel that I was born old. I really didn't stop to consider how old I have always felt until I retired. Hopefully, my growth of awareness will continue until I begin to lose what little mind I have left.

Perhaps I'll find a few more answers before I finally cash in all my chips.

Nevertheless, I'd like to share with you what I now remember, and perhaps put that remembrance into some perspective. The central characters are a group of Hawke folks and their friends whose exploits covered the past six generations. My tale begins with my great grandfather, Rock I. Hawke, who was a Civil War hero, and also an outlaw.

The names of people in this retrospective are all bogus, but most of the stories and some of the place names are true, or as authentic as my memory has allowed them to be. This re-naming of characters was done as much to protect the guilty as well as the innocent. Most importantly, it was also done to protect me from lawsuits.

There are a million stories on the naked prairie and nude mountains of Colorado. There is considerable

truth in all of the tales which follow, and, sometimes,
an occasional small lie.

1. A HARD MAN

"You worthless yellow-bellied rebs couldn't find your ass with both hands. I didn't steal nuthin'. Evidently you don't know who you're dealing with here. I'm a god-damned hero." The grizzled old man was sitting on a tall roan horse with his hands tied behind him. He choked back some tears.

"Well, either whup this beast out from under me, or shoot me in the head, you dirty bastards!"

According to a lawman, who was in the posse that hanged my great grandpa and who claimed that he had seen whole affair, these were the last words my great grandpa whimpered to this world. A Missouri sheriff slid a noose around his neck, whipped the roan on his backside, and the old fellow swung into eternity.

That incident may have been the second most important moment in that fellow's life. Perhaps the most significant time happened on a Civil War battlefield in Mississippi in 1863. On that occasion this same irascible man happened to be leading a ground charge toward what seemed to be certain death from the rifles of a large Confederate detachment.

"Nail that tall, flag bearer!!", came the cry from the confederate breastworks at Vicksburg.

My grandpa told me that Rock Illinois Hawke was a craggy-faced man with raptor-like eyes, a shaggy black beard, and a long, thin, athletic build. His escapades have been written about in various American history books, but this is the story I heard from his son, my grandfather, Long Jack Hawke.

I believe that my great-grandfather's life demonstrates many of the Hawke family qualities and weaknesses. On many occasions, he was a silly ass fool. In other situations, he appeared to have intelligence and courage. From what I've heard, I believe that he was a sometimes hero, and at most other times, an incorrigible, mean drunk.

My Grandpa said that the last time he saw his father, the old Rocker, as his drinking buddies called him, was wearing high lace boots, duck pants and an ancient blue union coat covered with medals and ribbons. He said that his old man was sitting in a rocking chair on their front porch, evidently lost in his revelry and talking softly to himself. Gramps said that his father was undoubtedly intoxicated again, and probably dreaming about the glories and debaucheries of another time.

Grandpa always ended his stories about his father with the line, "He was a hard son-of-a-bitch." It has been my experience that many other folks have said the same thing about later generations of Hawke men. Grandpa also said that although he couldn't understand why, most people seemed to like the old soldier a good deal. My grandmother had said on many occasions that R.I. was probably the most worthless character in God's creation, but Grandpa maintained that there was something fascinating about the old coot.

This is the main story he told me: Late in 1831, Rock Illinois Hawke was born the son of an Irish immigrant farmer in Franklin County, New York. He grew up to become a young a ne'er-do-well, and wandered about the northeastern United States until the age of 29, doing little but gambling, drinking, and whoring. Then he apparently decided to change his luck and his life-style.

He moved out west to Illinois where he married a pretty, seventeen-year old Welsh girl named Hattie Wilson. In the after glow of that occasion, Rock evidently believed that he might become a farmer and a responsible man just like his own father had been. He

Claude M. Higgins, Jr.

immediately got his young wife pregnant (many years later, he became an expert at this function), but not much later he lost his sense of responsibly and left her after just six months of marriage. He ran away from the hard work of supporting a wife and a child and enlisted in the Union army.

Up to this point he hadn't appeared to be socially conscious, but after becoming a soldier, he reportedly spoke out against the injustices that he felt were being done to black men and God.

His neighbors used to say that my great grandpa had an alligator mouth and a canary ass. I don't know for sure about that. I'll tell you the rest of the story and let you Judge for yourself. One year later the fellow found himself outfitted as a private in the infantry of the 99th Illinois, a detachment of volunteers which had been blended into the Union Army of the West. In the very few letters which he had written home to his wife, he had said that the subject of death was always on his mind now. He wondered what it would be like to die, and if he had the courage to face that event.

On the other hand, it seemed that he had also begun to wonder if there really was any reason he should continue to live his miserable, non-productive life. He told Hattie that "living was so damned complicated and demanding," a fact I feel certain that she'd certainly already discovered in trying to run a farm in his absence. On that fifth of June, l863, he was in a Union company attacking the Confederate lines at Vicksburg, Mississippi. According to the military record left by the Union commanding officer in that battle, R.I. Hawke was described as "a big, strong, stubborn, Irishman to whom I gave a great responsibility." Later events show that he also must also have been a cocky, tough scoundrel.

As it happened, the Union flag bearer had been shot through the head in the initial Union charge at the Confederate breastworks early that morning, and Rock begged his commander, Captain W.C. Johnson, for a chance to carry Old Glory on the next assault. In what must have been a moment of complete desperation, his Captain gave him the flag along with this order, "Don't you dare stop, you Irish bastard, until you get into the Confederate lines."

With a mighty holler, Hawke leaped over his own breastworks and ran forward toward the Confederate lines. His rough, Irish face under the little blue cap probably looked more than a little ridiculous, but that fellow was sprinting bravely through the smoke and withering fire of that battle field, and two hundred Union infantrymen were following him. He seemed determined to do something right in a life which had hardly been notable to that point in time.

The Union charge was met by the roar of five hundred Confederate rifles and a few old assorted muskets, but the Yankee soldiers continued to follow their flag bearer into that hell of bullets and death and toward the defenders of Vicksburg. As the charge neared the breastworks, the Rebel firepower reduced the union men to a mere handful. Just twenty-five yards from the Confederate line, Rock Hawke was the only Union soldier left up right. He was still carrying the flag and running as fast as he could directly toward the blazing barrels of the Confederate infantry.

Charles Perkins, a Confederate soldier in the Vicksburg line on that day, recorded in his diary that "A hundred men took deliberate aim at this crazy fellow, but he kept coming, and, amazingly, not a single bullet hit him." Suddenly all Confederate rifles ceased firing. A Confederate officer in the line of defenders stood up and shouted "Don't shoot that man. He is too brave to be killed just now." As soon as his Confederate comrades understood their captain's order, a hundred old gray caps and hats went into the air, and a hundred voices began shouting "Come on you brave, stinkin' Yank. Come on!"

Private Rock Illinois Hawke was taken prisoner, and brought before the Confederate general, W.W. Brightside. The general asked him to reveal his rank and outfit, which Rock answered with a smirk, "Rock Hawke from Illinois, your majesty, and up your rebel fanny."

"You're a smart ass," said the general.

"No," said Rock, shaking his head. "That's my god-damned name, and you're a damn gray-bellied rebel."

"How many men has your general got?, asked Brightside.

"Ten thousand more than you or any rebel general could ever imagine, said the fiesty Hawke.

The Confederate general then asked, "Where is Grant?"

"Don't you worry about Grant," said R.I. "He will be here tomorrow to nail you bastards up in a box and ship you back to our big boarding house in Illinois."

Brightside leaped up from his chair and shouted, "Get this Yankee soldier out of my sight before I run him through." Most luckily for him, Old Hawke was involved in a prisoner exchange just two weeks later, and was returned to his regiment along with a written message from the Confederate commander recommending this tough, obnoxious soldier for the Medal of Honor. His accompanying communiqué read, "He is incredibly obnoxious, but also a very brave man."

Amazingly, this incredible letter was written and exchanged between enemies. as a result, our nation's highest military decoration, the Medal of Honor, was awarded to R.I. Hawke on the battlefield of Mississippi by General Grant himself.

A few weeks later my great-grandfather was wounded and mustered out. He returned to Illinois and the wife he had deserted three years earlier. He discovered that Hattie had lost that first baby, but somehow she had managed not only to survive, but also had bought ten additional acres of good farmland which was to become the Hawke Farm for the next twenty years. Rock tried, but could never become a good farmer. Mostly, he just sat drinking whiskey on the front porch, always wearing the old Union blue coat with its chest full of decorations. He dreamt of escaping from this difficult farm life.

He played poker at night, and chased his wife in between times. My great-grandmother Hattie managed to keep them afloat by raising vegetables, chickens and strawberries. In 1880 when Rock was nearly fifty years old, they had their first child who was to become my grandfather. Then this couple produced nine more children in the next fourteen years. It seems as if it always takes Hawke men a long time to learn how to do things right, and then they, invariably, ride their new skill to death.

Rock couldn't handle all this productivity and responsibility, so once again he deserted his wife and their now ten children in 1894 when he was 63 years old. Within months of his departure, rumors occasionally made their way back to the Illinois farm where his wife and eldest son worked hard taking care of all the children and trying to make the farm a success. These rumors told about a man who had taken up with a gang of desperados in Missouri and become a cut-throat horse thief.

Official word reached the Hawke family some years later that Rock Hawke, Medal of Honor winner, had been hanged as a convicted criminal in the state of Missouri in late April of 1890. He was finally free of responsibility, and now, probably, is rocking his way through eternity.

2. IRELAND AND FRANCE AND MY SUMMER LIBERTY

My grandfather was Irish and my grandmother was French. Long Jack and Lucy Hawke raised three children. My father was the eldest. Pop had two sisters, Jean and Betty. Jack had been a farmer, barber, hardware dealer, and entrepreneur during his life time in the states of Iowa and Colorado. Lucy, my Grandma, was a high-spirited French lass with her finger in everything that went on in western Iowa. She was a bouncy high-spirited lass with dark eyes and hair. My grandparents were remarkable people who made great contributions to the society in which they lived.

I spent summers from first through sixth grade enjoying a temporary emancipation from my nuclear family. It was on visits to them that I learned the most about the realities of business, politics, the birds and winged stingers, small town societies, and most importantly, morals and ethics. My annual visits of three months flew quickly by, and it was with a certain reluctance I returned each fall to the Colorado prairie.

Grandpa Rock Iowa Oyster (called Long Jack by his friends) was a feisty Irishman with twinkling blue eyes and a great sense of humor. He had a sturdy build and a fine, strong jaw. Many people thought that he looked just like a tall Irish leprechaun. He had master horse-trader's sense for getting on in life. He knew every thing that was going on in the Missouri Valley, and everyone who made it go, and if there was a bargain anywhere, he bought it.

When he was fifteen and the oldest in his family, his father, a Civil War Medal of Honor winner, was hanged as a horse thief. Long Jack then assumed the support of his family of a mother and thirteen brothers and sisters. By the time he was sixteen, he had put himself through barber's college and owned twelve barbershops up and down the Valley.

In his late twenties he married Lucy, my grandma. They were a usually happy couple who lived together more than sixty-five years. Religion was important to their lives, and both attended church regularly. Grandpa knew what the laws of good conduct were, and although he didn't always accomplish them, he constantly aspired to them and taught me to do the same.

Each year in late May (between 1941 and 1946) I climbed onto a bus for the sixteen hour trip to Iowa. The differences between Iowa with its curbed asphalt highways and luxuriant farm fields, and Colorado with its mostly gravel prairie roads and dry land hills and washes, had a dramatic impact on me every time I made this trip. On these early bus trips, I saw con-artists, hustlers, and prostitutes at work, and one time in Omaha, I saw a black man with his throat cut dying on the sidewalk in front of a bus terminal. This was very heady stuff for a grade-schooler from the Colorado outback.

My grandparents always made over me when I got to whatever little Iowa valley town they happened to be in each summer. Grandpa usually had a horse for me to ride, and Grandma established <u>no</u> hours or perimeters - I had the run of the county. For six glorious summers I spent my time in Gramp's barber shop, or riding a horse, or working street carnivals that moved up and down the Missouri, or telling tall tales to the little Iowa girls about how I lived with the Indians out in Colorado. It was a perfect life for a little fellow.

My grandfather, in addition to being a one-man Irish mafia, was a very good pool hall gambler. I can remember standing in the pool halls, watching him play poker when he should have been cutting hair, selling radios, or at the least, home for supper. Grandpa also raised hogs, chickens, and strawberries. This combination of activities made him one of the richest men in southwest Iowa. In his later life, he got into real estate, but prolonged illnesses and a series of nursing home stays for both himself and Grandma reduced him to being a near pauper when he died at the age of eighty-eight.

I always enjoyed watching his business transactions. He displayed a low profile until he felt the iron was hot, and then he moved in quickly for the kill. I remember many of his famous deals.

One of these deals deserves telling about. Near the end of WW II he learned that a train-load of binder-twine had been pitched into fields and barrow pits in central Iowa at the time of a train derailment. Dealing with an over-whelmed insurance adjuster, he got the salvage rights for fifty cents a bale. Grandpa borrowed all the trucks he could talk nearby farmers out of, hired high school boys as drivers, and then moved several railroad car loads of twine into the big barn at the back of his property in Odebolt, Iowa. Binder twine had been impossible to get during the war. The farmers around Odebolt were ripe for Grandpa's product. He sold over ten thousand bales at ten dollars a shot. I asked him how much profit he made on each bale, and he replied, "Enough."

He was also a great trader. The depression years, a time when people didn't have the cash to pay for anything, had allowed him to fill sheds on the farm with bushels of corn, and the stock pens with hundreds of hogs that the farmers had been using as barter on haircuts and radios. Somehow, he always managed to unload these commodities when the market prices were highest. He was a real back- woods financier.

My grandmother was a tall, strong, pretty woman. She cooked, cleaned, and did a great deal of church work. Her fried chicken was known throughout Iowa. She was an expert seamstress, and homemaker. In later years, she worked side by side with Grandpa in a series of hardware stores, and still kept up all her domestic home duties. She had a dark beauty that stayed with her until her death at eight-five, great wit and charm, and the quickest tongue east of the Missouri. She and my Grandpa were like oil and water, their arguments sometimes lasted from spring to well into the fall. They fought about everything, but somehow they stayed together.

She told me one story of their courtship. She said that Jack would come in the evening to walk her through some nearby woods. Lucy's father, carrying a lantern, always accompanied them on these courting walks. She said that they both prayed for a foggy night on each of these courting walks. What a difference a century makes.

Long after they were both dead, I finally understood the great love they must have shared. I also realized that they were American archetypes. They had been some of the people who made it possible for the rest of us to live as we do in this greatest land in the world.

Their last years were spent in a nursing home in Fort Darwin where they had come to live in their old age near their oldest child, my father. My own little family visited them there whenever time allowed. I was always very grateful that my children were exposed to a little of the charm of these two great old people. I was also most thankful that, as a child, I had been allowed to share a little of their lives

3. TRASH MAN

Bill Ormsby was Ft. Darwin's entire trash removal department for all the years I spent growing up in that small prairie town. This old man with his horse and wagon was one of the last elements of our community to finally surrender to the twentieth century.

I watched the old fellow with the ratty straw hat drive his ancient high-sided trash wagon up and down the alleys for twelve years. The wagon was always pulled by two very old, brown horses whose ribs showed pitifully through their skin. Everyone in town said that the old man's horses should be taken away from him as their neglect was perfectly obvious to all. However, no one ever did anything, so this seemingly sad spectacle went on and on. Some old timers had told me Ormsby had been collecting trash just that way as long as they could remember. The old fellow died when I was eighteen, and the horses and wagon disappeared from our alleys forever.

I think that I was one of the very few people in our town who ever exchanged more than a sentence with the old trash man. My dad gave me three rabbits when I was eight, and told me to go into business. For the next five years I became the rabbit entrepreneur of the plains. My old dog and I caught a dozen wild rabbits to add to the original three, and within a year, and with the good will of nature and two over-sized bucks named Bugs and Thumper, my does had scores of bunnies.

Within three years, the permanent rabbit population had grown to three hundred, and that was even considering the fact that we killed, skinned, and either ate or froze about ten rabbits a week. Dad and I spent many Sundays building hutches to house this ever-growing population. I spent an hour each morning, and two after school, feeding, watering, and cleaning hutches. Soon we were slaughtering enough rabbits to sell rather large consignments to our local grocery store for re-sale to the public. I also learned how to skin the lovely beasts, and then salt and dry those beautiful rabbit hides. The sides of our barn were usually covered with the drying brown, white, and black skins of my rabbits. Old man Ormsby, the trash man, was the buyer for my by-product.

Once a month I would tie the dried skins into a bundle, tie that unwieldy package on the back of my bike, and make the trip down the hill toward the river to sell the skins at Ormsby's junk yard. The old fellow paid me 25 cents per skin, and then he would re-sell them to our local glove factory for twice that amount. I guess that I was never smart enough to eliminate the middle man, and, as things turned out, I really looked forward to my visits to the junk man.

On these monthly selling trips, I learned that the old trash man was quite articulate. I learned that he really loved his two old horses, and that the animals lived in a grassy meadow just above the river and weren't being starved to death. I discovered that his wife was dead, that he lived alone, that he had two grown sons who he had put through college, and that he was a much more solid citizen of our community than nearly anyone else in town realized. I found out that his two barns were full of the most amazing antique furniture I had ever seen. He said that people just threw it away, and that it should be somehow saved rather than just discarded, but I don't think that he ever sold any of it.

After his death, I often wondered what happened to all those treasures of antique furniture. He also had a dug a pit into which he threw garbage, grass, tree limbs, leaves, and field waste. He then sold this compost to people to use as fertilizer for their flowerbeds and lawns. He was a man far ahead of his time in the trash disposal business.

He seemed to look forward to these rabbit skin days as much as I did, and always delayed my departure by giving me a can of pop, and telling me about his adventures for the past month. The horses and wagon business had been his career. He told me that he had taken over the business from his father, and that he would be Ft Darwin's trash collector until he died. He was right. It wasn't until after the old man's death that our community bought two big trash trucks, and created the municipal sanitation department. I always thought that it was amazing that as civilization evolved, things got considerably more complicated, and that the simple solutions of our past were usually forgotten, and, invariably, replaced with much more complicated and more expensive procedures .

Old Ormsby had dumped our trash into a ravine near the bottom of his property. Today the city has four trash trucks, has employed ten men as collectors, and uses the same ravine as the site of the Platte County Landfill which they now have equipped with a great bull-dozer. All of this municipal structure accomplishes the same end for our relatively similar-sized population as Orsmby and his two bony horses had done for over fifty years.

My rabbit business helped pay for my first automobile - a 1941 Ford two door. The rabbits also provided my sex education without benefit of a public school curriculum. I asked my Dad, when I was eight, why the rabbits wrestled so much. He was trapped into explaining reproduction to me. Today I couldn't kill a rabbit if my life depended on it., and I have avoided rabbit skin lined gloves for many years. As a result of my knowing Old Ormsby, I believe that I am also just a little slower in judging people by appearances. I thank the old trash man/philosopher for that.

4. CONVERSATION

As a fairly young boy I had raised rabbits to supplement my income. It was a delightful job and hobby rolled into one except for the fact that once a month, we had to harvest. My father had driven a stout six-foot post into the ground and screwed a hook into that structure near its top. Usually about twenty rabbits were brought out one by one and slapped onto the hook by shoving the point of the hook through one of the rabbit's legs. Then their throats were cut, and they were skinned and gutted, their carcasses cut into pieces and frozen, their hides tacked onto a wall and salted and allowed to dry in the sun. Harvest day was always an incredible trauma for me. I was about eleven and still somewhat innocent. However, there were twenty-nine or so other days in the month which I found to be mostly wonderful with the rabbits.

It was nearly two years before I discovered an amazing fact about these little furry beasts. They have intelligence almost akin to humans! They think, they have mastered language, and they have developed a social conscience. Now I know what you, the reader, is thinking - Old Hawke has finally lost all his marbles. You can choose to accept the validity of this tale or not, but I believe that whatever way you choose to go with it, you will find it as completely astounding as I did.

One crisp fall morning I had gone out to feed and water my collection of approximately two hundred bunnies. My housing arrangement for this herd of hares was that I had built two large luxury compartments for the long-time studs whom I had named Bugs and Thumper, and twenty-five slightly smaller apartments for the breeding does in which they lived, had litters, and raised their families. All of this housing project was surrounded by a six-foot high dog-proof fence. In addition to the feeding, it was necessary to clean the hutches regularly, and line each hutch with new straw.

Their food was a mixture of vegetable waste that I collected from local grocery stores, and feed store pellets. Once every few weeks, my old dog and I would catch a few wild cottontails and jacks to add high-bred vigor to the domesticated group.

Now back to that fall morning. As I was feeding the does, I thought that I heard someone talking back by the stud apartments. I turned and looked, but there was no one there. Then I heard it again. I went back toward the noise, and there was still no one there. I stood looking into Bugs's cage.

The rabbit said, "I'm talking to you stupid. Don't you understand English?" Bugs was a great white rabbit who seemed to constantly wear a slightly malevolent expression. His pink nose and whiskers were trembling violently. His beady black eyes bored into mine. I stood aghast.

"You think we just sit here hour upon hour every day thinking about rabbit terds and sex? We do think a lot about sex, but there are other things in the world. By the way, how about throwing me into the pen of that gray Belgian down the line this week?" I remained speechless. "We can hear your damn too-loud radio. We know about the world."

Finally I found my voice. "I am indeed sorry, ur, Sir," I mumbled. I never presumed that you had the slightest interest in talking to me."

Bugs relaxed his posture a little. "Well, now you know. Since I finally have your attention, there are a few things that I would like to get off my chest. "At that moment there was a great thumping from the next hutch. Whack! Whack! It was Thumper revealing the reason for his name.

"Hey, you fellas," he said, "If you're finally going to have a discussion, I want to get in on it." The big black and white buck who lived next to Bugs was pushing his nose against the screen which locked him in.

"Hi, Thumper," I said. "I'm very glad that you're conversant in English as well."

"You're damn right I'm conversant. Who the hell do you think taught that white nut next door to talk?"

"Hold it . I'm first," announced Bugs.

"Fire away," I said. "The first thing I want to talk about is what seems to me to be a new, and totally erroneous definition of democracy," said Bugs.

"What do you mean," I asked.

Bugs began. "The last generation and a half of humans seem to think that they own the government. They seem to think that it was created just for them alone. What these self-centered idiots have forgotten is that democracy, your form of government, was created for all the people. It was created to guarantee them rights, but not ownership. They don't own it - they are responsible to it. Responsibility for the welfare of us all, or for that matter, any kind of responsibility seems to be an unknown concept to them. I think that it is about time that they got their ducks in a row, so to speak. And, I might add, you have the same responsibility to us. Since you have us penned up here, I think that you owe us protection and an explanation."

As I stood pondering that pronouncement, Thumper shouted. "Wait a minute. Enough about that stuff. I want to talk about rabbit business."

"Shoot," I said.

His bright eyes inditing my existence, he began. "I want to know what happens to our children when you take them out of here. I want to know what those terrible rabbit screams are. I want to know why we never see them again."

"Exactly," said Bugs.

After a moment of thought, I tried to answer his accusation. "There is the problem of population control. Like Bugs said, for the good of all, things must be done. I do give you food and water. I do provide you with living quarters. I do take good care of you."

He interrupted ."Shit," he said. "Don't give me any of that sociological welfare crap. What happens to our babies?"

"We eat them," I said.

Both rabbits stared at me and then turned and hopped back into the darkest recesses of their cages. I could almost sense what felt like a cold, black wind blowing through the enclosure.

"Let me explain," I said. There was no more sound from them and never would there be again. Our first, and only conversation was over.

5. FRONTIERSMAN

Old Sam was a rancher, mechanic, farmer, hunter, and authentic American frontiersman. Samuel Finley McGregor was born around 1895. He came to Platte County in the late 1930's and borrowed money to start a farm and ranch operation west of Ft. Darwin, Colorado. He and his family were friends of my family from 1938 on. I knew Sam and his wife and son during all the years that I lived in Ft. Darwin and spent many days visiting and working on his spread. He regaled me with many tales of the early days on the prairie. Unfortunately, I remember only a few of these frontier tales, but I can tell you a lot about the man himself. He was a short fellow, perhaps five feet, eight inches tall, but built very sturdily, and as strong as a horse. He always wore a somewhat quizzical expression on his face, and could not utter a single sentence without including at least several words of profanity. He smoked or chewed his cigars from daylight to bedtime, and seemed to be in almost constant motion.

As a teenager I helped Sam with his horses, cattle, and with the irrigation of his hay and sugar beet fields. Shortly before I left Darwin with my wife and children in 1967, Sam's wife of forty years, Addie, died, and he married a second wife, sold his farm, and moved high into the Colorado Rockies to open a small garage and work the rest of his days as a car and truck mechanic.

After supper each night that my family visited Sam and his family when I was a boy, the old man would squat against a wall and spend a couple of hours telling us about the current state of world affairs and what he experienced in the "old days." He had an opinion on everything, and seemed to be amazingly well-informed on all the topics he expounded on. I would have to say that these after supper lectures where we gathered on the linoleum in Sam's kitchen were a big part of my early education.

Sam fought an on-going fight with the powers that be in Platte County, and seemed to know not only what they had done to him, but what they did to everybody else who lived in that area of the state. He also spun stories about cattle drives, bear hunts, narrow escapes from cougar and wolf, coyote tales, rodeos, rattlesnake adventures, the development of the GW sugar factory, the Bijou Irrigation district, the introduction of cars and trucks into Platte county, great storms that he had experienced, the depression and FDR, commentaries on the changes in women's fashions, bar legends, stories about all the great people who had lived in or passed through the county, and an on-going evaluation of the local sheriff and police departments. Through the years, I listened with great fascination to all these amazing accounts.

I learned to drive a car in his hay fields, ride a horse on his prairie, set water in his ditches, shoot varmints near his creek and gulleys, milk cows in his barn, feed cattle in his lots, smoke cigars and cuss a lot, and eat incredible amounts of good ranch food prepared by his first wife, Addie. I felt that he was not only a source of wisdom, but also one of the first adult friends I ever had.

The last time I saw Sam was at my father's funeral. He was now nearly ninety years of age, walked with two canes, and was just a shell of the vigorous Cowboy I used to know. The twinkle was still in those bright 'blue eyes, however, and we hugged each other with tears in our eyes after we had buried my dad. I think that we both knew not only the sorrow of the Captain's death, but also the fact that it would not be long for Sam as well. We really didn't have much to say to each other. We just looked at each other with a small smile that assumed years of friendship. It had all been said and lived before. We also knew that a magic time we had shared in the 1940's and early fifties was long gone, and would never come again.

Later I heard that he had died in the mountains, that his son had become a big game hunter in Africa, and that the old man remained crustily confident, and tougher than a three-legged coyote right to the end. It could have been no other way for the frontiersman.

6. WOLF PACK AT THE FIREPOT

When I was about eleven, my family took our first real vacation. We decided to visit the famous Yellowstone National Park. The Captain, my father, my mother, and my eight-year old brother Bill, and I left Ft. Darwin for a five hundred mile trek to northwestern Wyoming. On the way up, my little brother caught a four-pound trout in a small stream near Pinedale, Wyoming. He was thrilled beyond words, and we all regarded his luck as a good omen for our journey.

We stayed the first night at the famous Yellowstone lodge near the geyser field in the Park, and were totally amazed by the incredible and colorful steaming pools, and the hot, roaring geysers. We saw the bears and moose of the park, up close and personal. I took several photographs of the bears, some by shoving the camera almost into their open mouths, a behavior which had caused my parents great consternation. We also were amazed by the beauty of Lake Yellowstone, its great blue expanse and its tree-lined shores creating a beauty that was unbelievable to prairie folk.

On the fourth day of our trip, my dad said that he wanted to drive up into Montana and see the Madison River, a world famous trout stream. For some reason, I was a brat that day, and said that I didn't want to go to Montana, but would prefer staying near the lake and fishing some of the little streams which emptied into it. I must have made quite a fuss, and at the age of eleven was obnoxious in the extreme, so the folks finally gave in and left me with my fly pole and a bag lunch near the Firepot River on the west side to the lake. Then they continued on their journey to the Madison. I was supposed to meet them at the ranger station near this stream at 6 o'clock that night.

Our old Chrysler was barely out of sight before I began to have second thoughts about facing this pristine wilderness alone. I was, however, eager to prove my manhood and my self-reliance, so I started fishing upstream, greatly enjoying the small river with its crystal clear water and the bright red and yellow stones which shone up through the water in the sun. The banks of this stream were high and rocky. Tall sweet grass sprinkled with tiny white flowers covered the bare areas near the edge of the banks. On the north side of the stream was a forest of lodge pole pine, thick and dark in its recesses.

After about an hour, I think that I was about two miles from the road where they had left me. I noticed a herd of range cattle in a meadow near the river. This was strange as cattle weren't supposed to be grazed on National Park land. Probably this small herd had wandered into the park from private lands in Montana. There was an old bull with a group of cows, and he seemed to immediately take exception to my presence. I edged out farther into the stream, and was watching tiny geysers, which give the stream its name, bubbling and hissing toward the surface of the water.

Then I had one of those strange feelings people sometimes get in the silence of nature. I felt that something or someone was watching me. I looked up from the stream toward the opposite bank, and almost dropped my six ounce fly rod into the creek. There, on a rise ten feet from the water, stood a pack of seven gray wolves. They were incredible creatures, strong and tall with beautiful thick gray fur, their ears erect and their yellow eyes all fixed on me in the middle of the stream. I couldn't believe what I was seeing, and for at least ten minutes both the wolves and I stared at each other without moving. In retrospect, I realized later that this time was definitely a magic time and I probably would never experience anything like it again. Both the wolves and I seemed to be frozen in that incredible time.

Finally the largest of the wolves, who stood in front of the other six, turned, and almost casually made her way back into the lodge pole. The other six wheeled and followed her. They vanished like smoke on a breeze into the timber without the slightest sound.

I fished back down the creek much more quickly than I had gone upstream, and was at the ranger station by noon. I told a ranger working there what I had seen, but he laughed, and said, "There haven't been any wolves in the park since 1930." My folks showed up before six, and I have to admit that I was very happy to see them.

Later that night, I told my dad about my experience with the wolves. Like the ranger, he also laughed, and said, "Sometimes little boys see things in the forest when they are alone that don't really exist. There aren't any wolves in Yellowstone."

But I know what I saw. It was I who looked deep into those yellow eyes. It was I that those wild animals were trying to communicate with. I even think that I know exactly what they were trying to tell me. "We are here. You don't belong here. What the hell do you think you are doing? Leave us alone and get out of our territory." Now, in 1998, the federal government is reintroducing wolves into this same area. Now it is the ranchers and a federal judge who are saying, "What the hell are you doing?" Isn't it amazing how attitudes change, and then, again, how they never change. The wolves are more real to me today than they were at that moment fifty years ago. I still see those yellow eyes sometimes at night. I think that they are still trying to tell me something more.

7. A FOREIGN AFFAIR

During WW II there was concentration camp for German prisoners of war in our town. Daily they were taken out of their encampment at our modified armory to work on the farms and ranches of the Platte Valley. Since there was a large native population of immigrant German farmers in our valley, it was inevitable that at least one of those young prisoners would fall in love with a local girl and she with him. Before I tell that story, however, let me describe that general situation in Ft. Darwin, Colorado, in the fall of 1944.

The war in Europe raged on, and thousands of German prisoners had been brought to the United States to be held in concentration camps until the insanity was to be over in 1945. Ten thousand such prisoners were assigned to Colorado imprisonment. Conventional prison Camps were built near Greeley and in several spots on the western slope of Colorado.

Ft. Darwin was to receive 500 such prisoners, but no great concentration camp was built here. Instead the county armory and its surrounding storage yards were enclosed by a ten foot wire fence, guard towers were built at the corners of the enclosure, and the German soldiers were kept right in the center of our village between the Conoco station and the city library. At night the prisoners would gather in front of the armory and sing to our population. They had strong, rich, male voices, and our whole community would gather in the street in front of the armory nightly to listen to their alternately sad or defiant Germanic songs. It was probably the best entertainment to hit our prairie town during the war years.

Ft. Darwin was an agricultural village that had depended on an influx of Mexican workers to serve as field hands every summer. The local farmers consequently welcomed the free field labor provided by the POW's. Farmers and ranchers argued over who would get detachments of these men every day that they were with us. As a young boy of our village, I was very interested to see what the Nazi horde looked like, and so took advantage of any opportunity to go over to the camp on a regular basis. It proved to be an experience that I would never forget.

The Main street merchants weren't as enthusiastic about this situation as were our agricultural inhabitants. Like all American prairie villages, we were, on the whole, extremely patriotic. War bond rallies, war stamps for the school kids, local air raid wardens, and fake air raids were a daily part of our lives during the war years. Hence, there was the development of a certain hysteria among some of our population when our local German farmers spoke their native tongue to each other in the stores. Most merchants would scream at them to talk "American." Since the merchants derived no direct advantage from the prisoners at our war encampment, and since there was an inherent social battle going on between the town folks and the farmers, naturally the merchants looked at the concentration camp as an ugly responsibility that disrupted what they perceived to be the normal flow of things. It also, they thought, excited our German population of American farmers. However, for us town kids, it was incredibly interesting. These young German prisoners looked just like our own young men. They didn't resemble the cartoon likeness of Adolf Hitler that we saw in our paper. For the most part, they seemed to be somewhat cheerful young fellows who were trying to make the best of a bad situation. I often wondered how these people could be guilty of the war crimes we read about. Could they, indeed, have killed our brothers, fathers, and uncles? Did the newspapers, the radio, and our parents tell us the truth about what was going on half way around the world?

A company of United States infantry had been assigned to guard these prisoners while they were in Ft. Darwin. To us these American soldiers were authentic heroes, but what puzzled me was that they looked and acted very much like the men they were guarding. The U.S. soldiers were everywhere around the concentration enclosure. Machine guns were manned at the street intersections around the armory. Ten armed soldiers accompanied every forty-prisoner detachment that was sent to work in our fields. The little of the war we saw in the newsreels at the Saturday dime movies seemed to be, partially at least, right here. My father, the "Captain", said that we shouldn't hate these German prisoners. He said that we shouldn't confuse them with Adolf. He said that they were just boys who were told to fight for their country, and most of them had done just that. There was one rather sad story, in particular, which came out of this period. The following is that tragic tale.

Prisoner Fred Stoller had grown up near a small agricultural village east of Berlin. He had been conscripted into the German army, sent to Belgium, and on his very first day in the field against the hated Americans, his company had been surrounded by the U.S. infantry, and Fred became a POW. When he was relocated to Colorado, he was just nineteen, and thought that he would never get back to Germany, and, as a consequence, felt very homesick. He was a tall, blond, young fellow who thought that his world had probably come to an end.

The first day that he was taken to work on Carl Weimer's farm, he noticed how much it was like his parent's farm in East Germany. When Carl's pretty eighteen-year-old daughter brought a bucket of water out to the beet field for the prisoners to drink, Fred thought that she was the most beautiful thing he had ever seen. She had bright blue ribbons tied in her fair hair, and a pretty green dress that revealed her strong, young body. Fred watched for her appearance every day, thereafter, as the prisoners harvested Carl's beets. Finally one day she was quite close to him, and he said "Good Day" to her in German.

Christina Weimer turned and looked right into his eyes."And a good day to you." she replied in his own language. For the next month both youngsters could hardly wait for their two-minute daily conversation. Then one day Christina slipped Fred a small package of biscuits. They seemed to be the best he had ever tasted.

Two days later he called to her when she came into the field with the water ration, and she made her way obliquely toward him so as not to raise the suspicion of the watching American soldiers. As she came nearer to him, her eyes grew brighter and brighter.

"If I could somehow escape when we load the trucks at the end of the day, and hide in that big irrigation ditch behind your barn, would you come to talk to me tonight?" Fred asked when she was next to him. Christina looked at the prisoner as if she had been waiting all her life for just such an invitation.

"Oh yes," she said, "But please, be very careful."

Fred did, somehow, manage to drop undiscovered in the ditch that day at sundown as the American soldier loaded the trucks to take the POWs back into town. He tried to lie without moving, but couldn't stop the fear rising within him. He waited for what seemed like hours, but then, suddenly, Christina was there.

At midnight he left her and started walking back to town and to the camp at the armory. He got nearly back to the Conoco station next to the armory before anyone noticed him. Then a young American soldier assigned to the machine gun at that intersection saw Fred's green prisoner uniform, and he knew he must do the job he had been trained to do.

"Halt," the young American guard screamed.

"What?" answered Fred. The staccato roar of the fifty-millimeter machine gun ripped through the prairie night, and young Fred Stoller lay dying in a pool of his own blood at the edge of the highway 6 &34 in our little town.

The war had really come to Ft. Darwin. The day after this incident, the attitude of our citizens had dramatically changed. The prisoners no longer sang for the American crowds at night. The local German farmers no longer spoke to each other in the German language while they were shopping in town. An atmosphere of fear and anger pervaded our community. The Weimer girl had told everyone that Fred had done nothing to her. They had only talked. She said he told her that the right thing for him to do was to go back to the camp. She felt that he had been murdered by the American army.

A sense of uncertainty and guilt was now to color our patriotism forever. It was to reach its full fruition thirty years later with the terror in Viet Nam. War is an incredibly tragic human situation, and the feelings it engenders can never be logically explained.

8. RENAISSANCE MAN

Aubrey Hugh Fletcher was my uncle on my mother's side of the family. He was also a second father to me during my youth. He had the best attributes of his Welch-English heritage, and was an accomplished man in many and varied fields. He was heavy set all his life, that is, until a massive heart attack a couple of years before his death at the age of 47. He was one of those people who lived at the wrong time as far as his weight was concerned. He really wasn't grossly fat, but he thought that he was. At his top weight, he was about 5'11" and weighed 210. Today, styles and tolerance for individual differences would have allowed him to live a normal life.

He was born about 1909, and in comparison with the long, lean Nebraska farmers he grew up with, he felt he was obese. This caused him to wear one uniform throughout his life. He always wore bib overalls to hide this shape. He never married because of his weight, but was a person full of love. He would have been an excellent husband and father. This tragedy of perception, on his part, is something that continues to haunt me thirty-five years after his death.

I spoke about the range of his talents. He demonstrated his excellence in studying and research, writing, teaching, bookkeeping, photography, singing, and merchandising. He ran a tin shop, an egg farm, a record store, was assistant superintendent for the Wyoming children's home, worked for the U.S. Post office, ran a boy's club, was an expert pattern maker and clothing producer, worked as a publicist for the Cheyenne Rodeo, and was a superior jewelry maker. He also was an outdoorsman. He hunted, hiked, and mapped much of the Wyoming back country. With all of these many interests and talents, he had a great deal to offer a woman, but he never had a romance. He felt that his weight made him unattractive to all members of the opposite sex.

I spent a great deal of time with Unc as a boy, and to me, he was certainly a model for my adult years. I spent many days working with him at all his various jobs, and innumerable evenings listening to his perception of living, and asking for and receiving his recommendations as to what I should do at various stages in my young life. I was particularly taken with his compassion and his love for life. He knew so much about everything but himself. This lack of self-confidence kept him from accomplishing the goals that I know he always held as dreams in the back of his mind.

Later, when I was married, I'm sure that he loved Summer and our children almost as much as I did. He must have been partially living out some of his dreams through my own family. He took thousands of photographs of our children, and spent as much time as possible both with my parents and my brother Bill, and with my own little family

When he died in 1960, I felt that my young life had ended as surely as if I had been in his place. My bother followed him into death a year later and Bill told me that he was going to live with Unc on a cloud. I really hadn't thought much about the possibilities of an after-life, but somehow that pronouncement made sense. Unc was a man for all seasons. We lost him before my own children reached their teen-age years. I have often thought about how much they missed by not having their uncle and grand-uncle around to offer some understanding and security during those turbulent times for them.

9. THE BEST OF THE BUNCH

Evie Gaberstone and Liz Hard taught at Fort Darwin High School for a combined total of eighty-three years. No one knew how many high school administrators and school board members they had outlived. Both women were unmarried ladies who became department heads and established the policies and standards of the Darwin school for a half of a century. They had educated at least two generations of Darwin citizens by the time I first hit their classrooms as a high school junior. I remember both of them seeming to be the most intelligent, poised females that I could then imagine. Evie was a Shakespearean scholar, and I was fascinated with the bard. I remember some of her lectures very well. One such lecture must have been heresy in Platte County.

"Shylock in Shakespeare's <u>Merchant of Venice</u> was a different sort of man than of the most ignorant bigots who became directors of that play have portrayed him to be for the last hundred years. I believe that William Shakespeare was a man far ahead of his time, and a writer far above the general intelligence of his audience and those who tried to interpret him. If you read the play carefully, you can see that Shakespeare presents his main character as a man who is racially, politically, and socially oppressed by the narrow minded Christians with whom he has to deal". I will never forget how this pronouncement by the woman on the podium in front of me was to later affect my own teaching, and my own future thought. However, at that point in my life, my first reaction was to think that this was heresy, and must be a damned lie. Her interpretation flew in the face of all that I had previously learned in my life. My parents and grandparents would have choked and sputtered if I had told them what she had said. I had heard a different story from them and many others earlier. "Jews must, in some way, be responsible for all our woes; they are a depraved people," was the common opinion of the prairie. She was a good presenter of material, and seemed always to end her lessons with the same expression - "We'll call that good."

Evie had gone to England for graduate studies following her graduation from Colorado University in the early twenties. Certainly, she was the best-educated and most sophisticated person in Platte County for many years. There were rumors that she had lost the love of her life, a young county farmer, to another girl. As a result of this misfortune, the legend goes, she had decided to forever remain an old maid, and to live most of the rest of her life with her mother.

Evie was a handsome woman who kept her hair tied back severely in a bun. She had a wardrobe of five different suits, one for each day of the school week. I remember her wearing the same five suits for twenty years. They must have been of remarkable quality. She appeared every day in hose and heels. She never shaved her legs, so the black hair curling and flashing through the hose destroyed some of her illusion of sophistication. She had a small stage built in her classroom, which, I suppose, was to remind her students, that she, after all, had seen Shakespearean plays produced at Stratford on Avon. Her voice was always well modulated, and she laced her speech with Elizabethan idioms. She demonstrated compassion for students in an era when such an approach was thought to be a sign of weakness. She was very easy to like. In retrospect of my long relationship with her, I must finally say, "We shall call that, and her, good."

Elizabeth Hard was an entirely different piece of work. Her appearance and demeanor struck terror into the hearts of her students, and even, occasionally, into the hearts of her fellow teachers. She was the daughter of Platte County farmers, and the sister of a long-time member of the Platte County school board. She fought bone cancer for the last twenty years of her life, and made weekly trips into Denver for radiation treatments. She was the toughest-minded woman I ever knew. You could never, ever, get ahead of her, perish the thought, or put her down.

She had an extremely sharp and penetrating mind and an excellent vocabulary, which made her an intellectual fount in the county. I remember some of the things she said which turned my world upside down. "Franklin Roosevelt and Harry Truman were two of the greatest presidents America ever had", and then, "The corruption of our government, and the lack of social equality in America can be laid directly at the feet of our conservative congressmen", or more startling, "It is not our grand army, but rather the United Nations that is our only hope for peace," and more, "Dwight Eisenhower is a military man who knows nothing about America's real problems. He would make a terrible president." Platte County was a hot bed of conservatism and reactionaries, but Liz was a full-blown liberal. As a rebellious young kid, I found her defiance of the establishment greatly appealing. Like her colleague, Evelyn Gablestone, Liz broadened the minds of thousands of Colorado farm kids. Her history, political science, and international relations classes were revelations to us all. "Think, think! Think!" she would scream at her classes.

Sometimes her dedication to a broader point of view got her in serious trouble with some of the influential citizens of our town. I think that she loved to fail our best athletes and musicians when they deserved to be flunked. Their removal from eligibility was too much to tolerate for some. However, Liz would not back down like most of the rest of us teachers, and the miscreants stayed flunked.

I never did well as a student in her classes in high school, probably because I had little self-discipline, and was myself, in a constant state of rebellion. I argued with her daily in class, buried cigar butts in her window geranium pots, played before-class basketball with her great globe, and in general, was a giant pain in the ass. But I loved that old woman. I was able to pass her classes because I left many a pair of freshly shot mallards on her doorstep. Many years later, and in her retirement, I remember that Liz came up to Windy Gap to visit Summer and me after we had moved to Windy Gap. It was an honor for us to have this grand lady visit us in the ramshackle little house we found to rent on our first year in the Gap.

Unfortunately, we too often forget the people in our past who have had a great affect on our lives. This is particularly true of teachers that we have had. Consequently, I hope that I am not alone in remembering a lot of what happened in the classes of Evelyn Gablestone and Elizabeth Hard - the best of the bunch.

10. COME TO SAFEWAY TO GET BREAD

For ten years I worked for Safeway in a great variety of jobs, both in Fort Darwin and in Windy Gap. I was, at various times, a produce man, a butcher, a night stocker, a checker, and a relief manager during my decade of affiliation with this national grocery chain. I came within a few minutes of, perhaps, spending my whole life with this outfit. When I graduated from college with an A.B., the Denver division manager came to visit me where my little family lived in a half Quonset hut in Vetsville at the University of Colorado, and offered me a job as manager of the St. Francis, Kansas, Safeway. The job paid four times as much as I could make teaching school, so I was sorely tempted. Summer told me that I would never be happy doing such a job, so I told old Hawk Hollingsworth, the D.M., thanks, but no thanks. In retrospect, it was both a good, and a bad decision. If I had taken the grocery job, my family would not have had the economic difficulties we faced for the first ten years that I taught. On the other hand, if I hadn't taught school, I would have missed a stimulating lifetime of study, and ten thousand interesting students and colleagues.

I began working as a produce flunky in Fort Darwin when I was fifteen. Safeway seemed to offer great opportunities for advancement, and paid a better wage than any other job I could have found at that time in my life. My long affiliation with them allowed me to get through college, and to help pay for the first few years of my marriage and fatherhood. I met a long line of interesting characters, and had some memorable experiences, so it was with a certain reluctance that I finally quit working as a grocery man about three years into my teaching career.

By 1952 I had worked in a fireworks factory, a drugstore, and had been day manager in an ice cream place. None of these jobs paid more than fifty cents an hour, so I was on easy street financially, when, at fifteen, I went to work for $1.40 an hour at the Fort Darwin Safeway. My first job allowed me the privilege of not only sorting and washing vegetables, but also the excitement of nightly mopping a huge tiled floor. My first manager, Robert Rawlins, was a philosophical old coot who put up with my incompetence, and at selected moments, taught me a great deal about how one becomes a man. Bob was a highly competent organizer of workers, and had enough compassion to be interested in us as people most of the time. I look back with respect to this fellow, and realize now that he was a better leader than many PHD superintendents I knew during my long association with the public schools.

Before long, I advanced to the position of assistant butcher in the meat shop, and began to learn something about merchandising. When I graduated from high school, I had an in at Safeway stores in the college towns which would be my home for the next several years. My job at the Windy Gap Safeway allowed my family to survive the first financially difficult years of my marriage, and when I returned to Fort Darwin to teach, my re-appearance at the Darwin Safeway supplemented my meager teaching salary to the point that we only had to borrow a hundred dollars a month in order to pay the rent and put food on the table. During the Windy Gap tenure, I became a night stocker, and then a relief manager for the middle managers during their annual vacations.

During these many grocery adventures, I met a large group of interesting characters. The first fellow who comes to mind was a character I met at the Fort Darwin store. His name was Elmo Tallman, and he was the most decorated G.I. in the Korean conflict. He was not a poised, confident man like Audie Murphy, the most decorated war hero of WW II, had been when I ran into that fellow once buying apples at the Windy Gap Safeway. When I knew him, Elmo was just a common sort of insecure under achiever, pretty much like all my colleagues at the grocery store. On Saturday nights after we had swamped the store floor, Elmo had taught us how to throw hatchets, and how to break one-inch pine boards with our hands. He had mentioned his record of accomplishment in the war, but it wasn't until one day when he brought a large plaque to work that we grasped his level of achievement. The plaque showed all his decorations, and square in the middle of the collection was the Congressional Medal of Honor. My great grandfather had also received this highest of our nation's military awards, and I was incredibly impressed that our assistant butcher had one as well.

Another acquaintance of my employment at the grocery chain was a seventy-five year old man named Lincoln Paisley, who may have been the toughest old man I have ever known. Old Linc rode his bike to work most days, only surrendering to a ride in his wife-driven thirty-eight Dodge on particularly stormy days. He could work physically harder than any of us young bucks, and was strong as a horse. He had thrown my 200 pounds on top of an eight foot high pile of canned goods cases on a couple of occasions, and could lug a side of beef of beef from the refrigerator trucks to the meat lockers in the butcher job with apparent ease. He was the only one of us who didn't fawn with subservience when the store manager came around.

Old Linc was a man in all ways. Once when we were unloading a semi-truck load of watermelons, tossing them about ten feet from man to man in a long line between the truck and the produce storage room, we got carried away and started to sling the thirty pound melons with more than reasonable speed to each other. The next man in line to me was Old Linc. I threw a big California Grey a little too hard at him, and it came back at me with such velocity that I had no chance for a catch. It caught me high in the chest and knocked me a good six feet back and on my back as the melon splattered into pieces all over the back room. What a great old horse he was!

During my undergraduate years at C.U., I worked forty hour weeks during the school year at the Windy Gap Safeway so that my wife and I and our daughter could live in our half-Quonset in the school's Vetsville. During most of this period, I was a produce man and worked with a lovable middle-aged Italian man named Joseph Petrelli Joe was a sweetheart of a man who worked hard and was devoted to his wife and children. I don't believe that I ever encountered a fellow who was so extremely happy just to come to work every day. This good spirited man was the sort who did his own job, and then helped everybody else in the store do theirs as well. Joe was a model to me, the sort of well-adjusted person that all of us hope some day to become. As I was recently married and overwhelmed with becoming a husband and father, I always looked to Joe for advice as to how to handle my own situation. In his charming Italian accent, he would do his damndest to help me solve my current dilemmas.

The final character I remember well from those grocery days was a Lithuanian immigrant named Augie Zadok. Augie's father had been a medical doctor back in Lithuania when the Nazis invaded his little county in 1940. The family had lost their comfortable living, and had been forced to move into an inner city ghetto. Then the Russians pushed the Germans out, and Augie saw his Dad machine-gunned to death on their front door step.

Augie and his mother came to the United States as displaced persons in 1952, and his mother supported them by cleaning university restrooms while Augie pursued his dream of becoming an aeronautical engineer. Augie and I worked as the night stocking crew together for a year in Windy Gap. At two in the morning, we often locked the front door and walked a mile into town for a cup of coffee at an all night bar. On a Christmas Eve one year during that time, Summer, Spring and I were driving around on a snowy holiday evening, and decided to drop in and visit Augie and his mother who lived in a small apartment in a lower class section of town. They were poor as church mice, but welcomed our visit. Spring was barely two, and a pretty, sweet little girl. Augie's mother took a plastic reindeer off their small Christmas tree to give to my daughter. That reindeer still adorns our Christmas tree every year, and has now for about forty years. It was one of those moments in life a person can never forget.

The last time I saw Augie was about ten years after we both had graduated from C.U. I had brought a high school golf team back to Windy Gap for a tournament, and had parked them in the university cafeteria to chow down. They were still busy eating when I finished, so I took a walk around the old campus. I met a fellow on the sidewalk outside the Memorial center, and had walked past him, when suddenly I knew that it was Augie. He turned at the same moment, and after a bear hug, I discovered that he was at C.U. attending an aeronautical conference, and that he and his mother lived in Cinncinati where He worked for a large airplane design company. We temporarily renewed a friendship, which had sustained us both many years before.

The last thing I remember about those years at the grocery chain, was the slogan perpetuated by our assistant manager at Windy Gap. He reminded the crew daily to "come to Safeway to get bread." Good advice for those in the market.

11. STOVEPIPE CANYON

The cry of a mountain cougar seemed to echo down the canyon walls and reflect off the flashing waters. I could just see a splash of yellow fur from where I was casting my gray spider dry fly upstream above a small riffle on of the North Platte River in south central Wyoming. In 1952 My dad, "the Captain", and I took my Grandpa, "Long Jack", into Stovepipe Canyon on a remarkable fishing trip. It was a spring trip, which meant that the waters of the river were at about their highest point of the year.

This canyon lies about ten miles south of Encampment, Wyoming, where we headquartered, and ten miles north of the Colorado State line on the Platte. The side road through the A Bar A ranch, is unpaved and rocky, and from the highway, takes some thirty minutes of negotiating rocks, cattle guards, and barb wire gates to reach the spot where you can park your car and begin a thousand yard walk into the river itself. At that point in the canyon the river divides around small islands into one hundred-yard wide channels with the water averaging about two and a half feet deep this time of year. There are some holes of ten to fifteen feet in depth which crater throughout the main flow of water. Most anglers boat through the river at this point, but the three of us decided to fish it from the water itself.

The force of the rushing water is such that you must constantly be fighting to maintain balance when you are in the channels. The rewards for all this trouble and effort are fourteen to eighteen inch Rainbow and German Brown trout that eagerly strike light brown or gray dry fly patterns cast upstream over their lairs. It is a wildly beautiful canyon with many great brown and gray rocky crags jutting from the walls of the canyon, and we had numerous sightings of mule deer, brown bears, and cougars on the banks and or on promontories jutting out from the walls. High on the sides of the canyon on that day, I had seen three cougars sunning themselves on rocky ledges. It was one of those great beasts, which had attracted my attention just a few minutes ago. This particular cat's scream had been so human-like that it had raised the hairs on the back of my neck. As I looked toward the ledge on which the cat stood, I saw a pair of golden eagles circling in the bright sky above. When we first reached that spot on the bank from which we wanted to fish in the river, we found the remains of dozens of mule deer which had not survived the previous winter. Grandpa spent the first thirty minutes collecting a pile of magnificent antlers, which he intended to haul back to Iowa to amaze and delight his farmer neighbors. We got them back to the car that evening, but the horns, in addition to our fishing gear, gave us a hell of a load.

We decided to wade the first channel and try fishing the far bank from an island directly opposite our entry point. We were just twenty feet into the water when we were surrounded by literally thousands of water snakes which had evidently washed down from somewhere up stream. Although these reptiles are relatively harmless, that many of anything is rather threatening. When we reached the island, we realized that that ground was covered with more thousands of these snakes. Grandpa was near hysteria as we struggled across this slick land surface and headed out into the middle of the second channel. We found a rocky area where the water was about eighteen inches deep, and from that point began to cast our dry flies up stream and let them be carried by the fast current past holes and rocks where big trout had to be waiting. The fishing was absolutely magnificent, and soon our creels were heavy with fat trout. I hooked into a four and a half pounder, verified later by the scales in Slim Allison's cafe, that fought me for about twenty minutes before I could finally get him to the net. He was too big for the creel, so I hooked a large barb through his jaws, and tied him to my belt where he hung, his tail reaching below my knee.

It was getting dark by that time, and we had to start back to the car. That meant negotiating the two channels and the red-rib water snakes once again. The Captain, my father, and I reached the island first, and looked back to see Grandpa thirty feet out and struggling to get to us. We headed back toward him, and when we reached him, handed him our rods, and with one of us on each side, he wrapped his arms around our necks, put our shoulders under his arm pits, and we started for the island. The rocks on the riverbed always seem somehow to get slicker in the late afternoon, and we slipped and slid back toward the island. Sure enough, the red rib serpents were still there.

We quickly made our way through the writhing snakes, and then slowly traversed the first channel back to the bank where a path led to the point where we had parked our vehicle. For years afterwards, Grandpa Ray would tell people that he had carried both of us to safety across the Platte at flood stage on that memorable fishing trip.

Once you are out of the rushing, noisy river, you can notice the great savage beauty of the place. As we knelt on the bank in the gathering darkness about fifty feet apart cleaning our fish, I was aware of the incredible bright gold and red of the sky in the west beyond the canyon rim, and of the lush green meadows broken by growths of willow bushes stretching back from the river. The sky was soon full of circling and gliding eagles who somehow knew of our activity, and soon they were landing on rocks ten feet from us where we hurled fish innards toward their eagerly awaiting claws and beaks. The great birds put on a noisy show of wing-flapping and screeching as they gobbled the delicacies of trout innards. Suddenly the eagles near my fish cleaning spot lifted into the air, and I looked back at a huge brown bear just ten feet behind me on the bank. With a howl, I dropped my fish and headed back into the river. The Captain and Grandpa immediately saw my dilemma and started throwing rocks and heavy willow branches at the bear. Luckily, he was in no mood for a conflict, and ambled slowly back into the willows.

That night we celebrated at Slim's cafe with a two-pound rib steak and four cans of cold beer each. The fish were in Slim's freezer, to be ready tomorrow for our return trip to Fort Darwin. It had been a great day,

It should have ended that way, but upon our return to the cabin, I decided that one thing I needed to do was teach Grandpa how to play poker. The old fellow cooperated with much chuckling, but without saying a word. After thirty minutes of my inept instruction, the Captain reminded me that his father was probably the best poker player in Iowa, and had had that distinction for more than three decades. Oh, to return to the great joys and ignorance's of my teen-age years. More importantly, just to see those two fine people once again, and talk with them about Stove Pipe canyon and all the creatures that live there.

PART TWO
TEACHING IN FT. DARWIN

Claude M. Higgins, Jr.

INTRODUCTION TO PART TWO

My first teaching assignment, one lasting ten years and beginning in the fifties, was in the town called Ft. Darwin. During that period in my life, I established a family and learned to survive as a public school teacher.

Ft. Darwin is a prairie berg which can be found in Northeastern Colorado nestled deep into a long valley along a river called the South Platte, a river which runs in a diagonal direction northeast toward the Nebraska border. This small town is representative of many of the towns which have erupted along the front range of the Colorado Rockies in a line from Wyoming to New Mexico. True, Ft. Darwin is some distance from the Rocky Mountains, but you can still clearly see their peaks rising to the west. The South Platte valley is marked by bluffs, and buttes, washes, gullies, and springs nesting in the sand. Mesquite and sage brush, huge cottonwoods, willows, wild current bushes and cattails fringe the river and melt into the buffalo grass of the plains.

Many times I floated this river on a raft and at other times, hunted its bottoms. In the process, I discovered that this area is home to bison, pronghorn, mule and white-tail deer, badger, beaver, coyotes, wild horses, bob cat, Jack and cottontail rabbits, American and Golden eagles, pheasants, quail, many species of ducks, geese, red-winged blackbirds, meadowlarks, red-tail hawks, rattlesnakes, bull snakes, river turtles, sand turtles, lizards, catfish, carp, and suckers (both human and aquatic), and a whole passel of strange and wonderful human beings. In other words there are more damn things to look at, talk about, hunt, and eat than you could shake a snake at. This horn-of-plenty was what brought the Indians (Arapahoe, Cheyene, and Kiowa) into this valley. It was what later brought the soldiers and settlers and merchants. It was what brought the railroad, the ranchers, and the sod-busters.

It was what made possible Ft. Darwin, that beaver lodge of human habitat.

A common misconception is that the people who live here are yokels. That's only partially true. In fact, many of the inhabitants of this area are more interested in, and know more about, what is happening in the world than do most inner-city people. Many are very well educated and sensitive to the problems, which face humanity.

Of course there are others who are stupid, petty, vicious, and self-serving. I guess that I would say that the prairie is the real heartland of America and representative of all our nation's strengths and weaknesses. In other words, this area has its our share both of heroes and of fools.

The small city of Ft. Darwin itself perches on bluffs high above the South Platte. Its history goes back to Indian-fighting days as it was an outpost for pioneers seeking protection against the Indians who had lived there for almost one thousand years. The Indian people, in turn, sought protection from the white-eyes' invasion by attacking them at every opportunity. The native Americans naturally lost the control of the area, but I don't believe that their centuries of spirit and culture ever left this remarkable place.

By l930 the town had become an agricultural center. Oil was discovered in areas on every side of the community, and the population zoomed to about 7500 by l950. Much later, a small community college gave it some educational validity. Like most small towns in our country, it became an amalgam of people and life-styles. Ft.Darwin is 75 miles from the capital of Colorado, Denver, and, some say, 75 miles away from real civilization. The town is laid out symmetrically with broad avenues branching off from an inter-state highway. One town wag suggested that it was a town with "broad streets and narrow minds." I think that it is, and was, more than that.

12. TERMINAL ENGLISH

There was a class I taught once which some wag in the scheduling office called Terminal English because it was a class designed for those seniors who couldn't make it to graduation in regular classes and had no plans for college.

One Black Monday after Easter break this class suffered a great trauma. The daffodils and iris had burst into their full glory as on cue for the holiday. The sun was bright, and the grass had taken on that special green that comes only with Spring. The students filed into the room quietly, and I felt that at the start of this beautiful spring day, something was terribly wrong. They were all far too quiet. I was taking the roll for my eight o'clock class from the seating chart on my podium and noticed that all the students in row one were absent. I had set up the classroom in five rows of six chairs. Six students gone from one row was highly unusual.

"Does anyone know anything about all these absences?" I asked the class.

A pretty little blond girl in the one of the front chairs (a girl, by the way, who didn't really belong with that particular group) said, "Mr. Hawke, there was a terrible accident Saturday night." She didn't say anymore.

"What happened?" I asked. Silence was my answer, and I now began to feel a great apprehension.

Finally a tough farm lad I had good rapport with said, "They all were killed in a car wreck on seven-mile corner Saturday night. They were drinking, .. goin' too fast, .. missed the curve, .. wiped out the horse corral at the corner." In retrospect I can't remember what happened the rest of that hour. I know that felt a kind of horrible detachment from reality After school, my buddy, Crunch Carson, and I went to the Sheriff's impound lot to see the remains of the car in which the six students had died. It was a horribly twisted pile of steel, cloth, and blood. The faces of my now dead students flashed through my mind. Afterwards I had learned that the six who died had picked up a lad in a nearby hamlet before they took their dreadful ride into eternity. Seven young people, three girls and four boys, had been killed in an instant. Thirty-five years later, I still can't grasp the extent of my sorrow and shock on that day. Then, as now, the enormity of the personal tragedy for the families of these victims and for the community as well was almost too much to comprehend. I still haven't been able to accept what happened on that terrible Easter Eve. I always begin to remember some of the individuals in that group when this tragedy is reconsidered.

That terminal English class was filled with unforgettable characters. One such fellow was a tough Mexican lad named Rudy Garcia. He stood about five foot seven, and was put together like an Olympic wrestler. During our year together, Rudy and I had hit it off well, and he had appointed himself to be my bodyguard. At Halloween time, he came up to my desk after class and said, patting the area between his shoulder-a place where all the young Chicano boys carried their knives, "Mr. Hawke, if anyone bothers your house or you, let me know. I'll take care of them."

What Rudy lacked in intelligence, he made up for in loyalty and pure animal strength and cunning. He became a natural leader of the other Mexican boys at Ft. Darwin High School, and was responsible for organizing the annual Spring fight with the white-eyes. At noon on a particular May Day, about fifty Mexican boys annually met about fifty white boys in a fight in front of the high school. Weapons of choice were car jacks and bicycle chains. The fighting was usually bloody and vicious, but, thankfully, had not yet been fatal. Old Hawke, the teacher, had been in the middle of a couple of these altercations, as I had believed, fool-heartedly, it was part of my job to stop violence on the school grounds. Finally one of the old-timers on our teaching staff had taken me aside and said, "Stay out of those things. You could get killed."

Somehow, Rudy seemed to know of my dilemma. He said once, 'I know you care more than the others, but you really ought to stay away from the Spring fight."

I made it a point never to call on Rudy in class. It would have been too much humiliation for the junior patron to not know the correct answer in front of white farm boys. Rudy Garcia became the second Mexican-American boy to graduate from Darwin in the history of the school. On graduation day, it was hard to tell who was more proud - the Garcia clan or Rock Hawke.

Claude M. Higgins, Jr.

Two months after Rudy's graduation, he got into a fight at a festival being held one Saturday night at the Mexican Colony dance hall. This building was in reality an old implement shed ten miles west of town where young Chicanos gathered to dance and drink. Rudy stabbed another young Mexican to death in a dispute over a girl, and was sent to the Colorado State Penitentiary for life. A life term there for Rudy meant only two months as he was himself knifed to death in the exercise yard by a fellow inmate soon after matriculating.

Two other unforgettable characters in this same class were. Ashley Windham and Victor Carpenter, Jr. Ashley had achieved the reputation of being the town pump by the time she was eighteen. She was a pretty girl, but was already on the over-ripe side at the age of eighteen. She had beautiful long-lashed eyes, and pretty dark curly hair.

Vic (Jocko, as he was better known) was the playboy son of the largest cattle feeder in Platte County. He was a tall, almost-handsome lad with bright red hair. It was rumored that his father gave him $500 a month to stay away from the family business. At that time, that was $200 more than I made teaching school for the same period of time. Jocko earned his nickname because he had refused to cut the carrot-red hair, which had then surrounded his round face in huge airy curls.

I had had this pair in summer school for the two years before, and now had them together again in this regular year class designed by the district to rid itself of their ilk forever. They were both merry-makers, and came up with some entertainment for the class daily. Ashley wore outrageous clothes designed to stir up the hormones of all males within a mile of her, and Jocko roared up to school daily in his Cadillac convertible, much to the chagrin of all the other senior boys. Most of our senior lads had worked hard to come up with an old second-hand Ford pick-up, and that new Caddy was just too damn much. Ashley had appeared on my front porch in her skivvies late one summer night, and in the process, shocked my wife, Summer, into a two-day silence. Ashley also liked to call me around midnight from the local jail after she had been picked up by Deputy Sheriff Milo Cracker for an act of solicitation, and pleaded for me to come down and bail her out.

One day, at what must have been a particularly boring moment in class, Ashley started flaming a butane lighter. She eyed Jocko sitting in the seat immediately in front of her, and then, with a flourish, set his great halo of red hair on fire. I leaped toward the conflagration trying to throw my coat on Jocko's head.

Ashley was convulsed in laugher. Lester Work and Alfred Hardcastle, two dry-land farm boys who obviously detested Bozo's affluence, were standing up cheering on the flames. Victor Carpenter Jr. survived and re-appeared in class two days later to the cheers of his comrades. He now had a close red crew cut which exposed his unnaturally pink head. Ashley became a temporary heroine to the financially oppressed, and I vowed to never again agree to teach such a group as this.

Leonard Barnhouse was yet another of the colorful characters in this same class. Leonard was twenty years old, and still a senior. He was surly, sneaky, and generally an undesirable person. His rat-like face seemed to wear a perpetual sneer. His favorite occupation in class was making disparaging remarks about everything that happened, and bad comments about everyone else who shared his daily imprisonment on our classroom. His moment in the sun happened shortly before one Christmas vacation. He was mouthing off as usual; and I said. "I've had enough of you, Leonard. Get up and get yourself out of here."

Leonard stood up and glared at me. "Teacher, you are a son of a bitch, and you can go straight to hell."

There was a momentary stunned silence, and then I started for Leonard. Unfortunately, I knocked two girls and their desks over before I reached Leonard. In a fury that had been building toward this jerk for four months, I grabbed Leonard and threw him out of the classroom door. I was on top of him before he could get up off the floor. I kicked the boy to the top of a stairway and down two flights of stairs to the principal's office on the first floor. It was only as we tumbled into the administrator's office, that I suddenly realized that I had probably just ended my career as a public school teacher with my far too rash reaction.

Ordering Leonard to stay on the discipline bench and not move a muscle, I headed for the telephone. I felt a real fear now that my rage had calmed down somewhat. Naturally, Dr. Seldom Wright, the principal, was not in at that time. It was the same on that particular day as on nearly all others. (Seldom believed in engaging in the development of Main Street public relations during the school day. Someone else could run the school.) I rang Leonard's home, and the phone was answered immediately by his father. He must have been sitting on it.

"Hello" he said

I couldn't speak for a moment. What would he say when he learned about what had happened? Would I lose my job? Would criminal charges be brought against me?

"Mr. Barnhouse, this is Rock Hawke. I'm Leonard's English teacher. We had an incident in class today. He cursed me, and I'm afraid I lost it. I have just literally kicked him downstairs to the principal's office. I'm very sorry this happened. "

There was a momentary silence on the other end of the line, then I heard a deep-throated chuckle and then Mr. Barnhouse said, "Don't worry about it. I've wanted to do the same thing to Leonard for years. I'm only sorry that I wasn't there to witness it. I'll be in and pick him up in a few minutes."

"Thank you, Sir," I said as I hung up the phone, probably just a little short of a major heart attack.

Leonard and the six who died on Easter week-end were the only students in this class who didn't take their places in the graduation line that May. Teaching that class was one of the most memorable experiences I ever had, and now, thirty-some years after the fact, I don't know how I lived through it, but, in a way, it must have had its good moments as well. In any case, now that I have a little more perspective, I would like to try it all again, and also try my damndest to talk those six celebrants into staying home on that fateful Easter eve.

13. WRASSLIN'

It was time for the big match of the tournament - the state heavyweight championship. In their first period the two behemoths circled each other and feigned take-downs. No points were scored. As the second period began, the Denver wrestler, Will Hurt, roared out of his corner and grasped Ft. Darwin's Arch Watkins by the shoulders and neck, and tried to throw him to the mat. An audible gasp came from the throng of Darwin fans, but Arch locked his hands under Will Hurt's arms, and lifted him straight into the air. Two feet off the mat, Hurt's legs were thrashing, and he emitted a loud groan. Arch flipped him in mid-air and slammed Hurt's head and shoulders into the mat. The smack of Hurt's body hitting the plastic covered mat preceded the referee's three sharp slaps indicating the pin. Arch was state champ again, this time for the fourth and final time. He had been state champion every year since he was a freshman.

Wrestling was the number one spectator sport in Ft. Darwin for many years. The team won several state championships in a relatively short period, and always seemed to produce quite a few quality grapplers. The crowds that assembled in the Ft. Darwin gymnasium on Friday and Saturday nights were always vocal and intense. After all, this was "wrasslin". The type of folks who gathered for these matches were different from any other athletic crowd that came together in Darwin. Most of the male spectators wore the rancher -farmer uniform of bib-overalls or tight riding jeans, and the women all looked like someone's "cookin'-cleanin" mother. They started screaming for their sons and nephews as soon as they entered the gym. The Wrestling team members during the ten years I taught in Ft. Darwin were tough-as-nails farm-boys, sons of the Mexican colony, and town boys who worked hard and wanted a bit of the glory that surrounded our many state championship teams.

I remember well the many successes that this team accumulated during their reign of terror under the leadership of their great coach, Fog-Horn Smith. Year after year, they were conference, district and state champions. Coach Smith had finished his college career as the second best NCAA wrestler in his weight group in the entire United States. His voice was loud and deep. The loudest sound one heard during a Ft. Darwin wrestling match was Foghorn Smith's exhalting his wrestler to "come on", and 'stick "em". Out on the prairie, football and basketball are interesting, but "wrasslin" was the true measure of a young man's ability.

Long after I had moved to Windy Gap, Smith and his wrasslers continued to win every title in sight. I have often thought about the un-ending line of great wrestlers to come from Ft. Darwin, and how it could have been possible for a small town to produce so many very tough boys. The real secret for their success probably wasn't just all those rock-hard farm and ranch kids, but rather a coach who was a great teacher. Fog Horn was a fellow who had found a way to capture their attention and teach them those things that made a difference. Then, most importantly, he inspired them to reach greater heights than most teen-age boys ever dream of. Go figure.

14. WATER

Three primary liquids built Platte County - water, oil, and blood. I want to tell you about the first one. I'm not really smart enough to comment intelligently on the other two.

I never made enough money teaching school in the Platte County schools to support my family, so I was always searching for part-time jobs to supplement my family's meager income. One of the best summer jobs I ever had was bringing water from the great reservoirs twenty-five miles west of Darwin through an extensive system of irrigation ditches into the farming and ranch valley surrounding our little town. I did this for three years, in addition to, at the same time, teaching summer school to all those high school boys and girls who had failed regular year classes.

The irrigation procedure was as follows: a man known as a ditch rider was put in charge of maintaining a few hundred miles of inter-laced irrigation ditches. It was his job to keep them clean, burning out the weeds twice a year, removing the carcasses of dead animals who stumbled into the ditches, re-building the earthen banks which held in that most precious resource of water, and then in setting individual gates in concrete slots in order to let the correct number of acre feet of water into the parched fields of each farm and ranch. In addition to these duties, the ditch-rider had to take twice-monthly orders from each of his consumers for the amount of water they wanted. With all this responsibility, the ditch rider needed an assistant. I was his man.

Irrigation was the very life-blood of an agricultural area that seldom received more than a dozen inches of moisture in any given year. At three o'clock on two mornings a month, the senior ditch-rider and I would release hundreds of acre feet of brown, cold reservoir water into huge ditches that carried it eastward to its eagerly awaiting customers. The ditch-riders had to stay ahead of the flow, adjusting each landowner's gates and checks so that they would receive the correct amount of water. It usually took about fourteen hours to push the water and set all the gates in order to reach the end of our route, which stretched the length of Platte valley.

I had found this job through the Colorado employment agency where they instructed me to contact a man known as the head ditch-rider who would then give me more specific instructions. This fellow's name was Swede Dahlquist, and he and his wife lived in a small cottage south of the Burlington tracks in Ft. Darwin. I didn't know what to expect that early June morning as I drove into Swede's yard for the first time. The old man saw me coming, and was standing there when I stopped the car. "Boy, am I glad to see you!" he said as I got out of my wife's 1950 green Chevy coupe. We had inherited the car from my uncle, and had decided it would be just the thing for ditch-ridin'.

"We got lots of work to do," Swede continued as he climbed into the passenger side of the coupe. Swede was seventy and built like a bull. He had worked hard all his life and was still in good shape. Swede's pretty white-haired wife trotted from the back door of their small house and handed me a package of home-made cinnamon rolls wrapped in waxed paper. "You'll need these today," she said.

What a day that first ditch ride was! There seemed to be a million things to learn, and Swede gave me instructions on them all in the first three hours of our new partnership. We traveled twenty-five miles west to the Empire and Jackson reservoirs so I could see where we were going to get our semi-monthly water supply. Swede showed me how to open gates, how to measure great quantities of water in acre feet, how to shepherd the priceless liquid down the main ditches toward the Weldon and Ft. Darwin valleys, and then release parcels of it to our many farm and ranch customers. The old man explained how to get orders from individual customers, and how important it was to let them know you were coming, and when you'd likely arrive.

"They'll shoot anyone dead who's messing with their water gates unless they know it is the ditch-rider." I thought that this was an exaggeration, but found out later, he was right on the mark. That first summer I found this job to be the best temporary employment I had ever had. I got to meet lots of "real" folks, learned how hard life was on the prairie, and also how important water was to the survival of that culture. On every water run I had learned to expect farmers to meet me at their land boundaries. Some of them lived many miles from Ft. Darwin and didn't get into town very often. In addition to bringing them water, I became a regular guest to them and their families. I ate meals, drank lemonade, listened to all the news about new colts and calves (the smaller children in each family always took me to the barn to witness these additions to their farms) and tried to answer a thousand questions about what was happening in town before I left them to move onto the next farm or ranch, sometimes five miles away.

Most of these folks were simple, poor people who were barely eking out an existence on the eastern Colorado prairie, but they were forever generous with their food and time. Over the years I ate a great many meals of good food while watching chickens sitting on nearby furniture, but I also experienced the prosperous ranches where I ate in dining rooms more spectacular than any in town. I had the added advantage of being a teacher. I had had many of the older children of these families as students in class, and these children were always excited about introducing Mr. Hawke to their parents and siblings, and in having me eat with them in their homes. Somehow my position as high school teacher made me something of an authority to these people. What they didn't know was that I was in awe of them.

There were several incidents that occurred during these three summers that I must tell you about. One hot June day Swede and I were burning ditches. The irrigation canals fill up with tumble-weeds and other debris during the winter and must be burned out before the water is turned into them in the Spring. The rig for accomplishing this feat was a five hundred-gallon propane tank on wheels pulled by a tractor along the ditch banks. One ditch rider (me) stood on a rotating platform on top of the propane tank wielding a long-necked flame-thrower down into the debris that had collected in the canals.

Swede drove the tractor pulling the tank and me. This procedure was hot and tedious and required that Swede keep the tractor upright, and that I burn everything in the ditches without incinerating our rig. Many times, small wild animals and reptiles were sacrificed to the flames in our attempt to clear the ditches. It took a good deal of strength to keep that long necked flame-thrower where it belonged. This fact was driven home on a particular June day as we were burning a large canal ten miles south of Ft. Darwin in the Adena area of Platte County.

Swede was driving the tractor on a narrow road atop a twelve-foot deep ditch. I had the burner going full blast over the edge of the embankment. The tractor's front wheels hit a soft spot, and the machine began to slowly tip toward the bottom of the ditch. Naturally, the wheeled propane tank began to tumble as well. Swede screamed at me, and leaped off the tractor just as it went over the edge. I was fighting to keep the burner off the tractor and Swede, but the old rotating platform whipped me around back toward our rig. I leaped just in time as the two vehicles crashed down into the deep irrigation ditch.

Swede and I landed about twelve feet apart and instinctively covered our heads with our hands expecting the whole damn thing to explode. It didn't, but it took two farm tractors two hours to get us out and running again. I feel that the God of the prairie must have been watching over us that day.

There are a great many rattlesnakes out in that county. As ditch riders we ran into more than our share. Two incidents are as clear in my mind twenty-five years after the fact as they were on those two days when I looked fanged death in the face. Ditch riders need to measure how gates are set and then insert boards in concrete checks in order to guarantee that each customer receives exactly as much water as he has ordered. One morning I needed to set such a gate which happened to be at the bottom of a five-foot deep check. Normally I carried a long-handled shovel both to repair ditches and to whack rattlers with. This particular morning I had left the shovel in the Chevy, and leaped into the check with only a yardstick as the water was coming quickly down the ditch behind me.

I landed on top of a six foot rattler who was damned angry about being trapped there in the first place, and even more angry when my two hundred pounds came down right on top of him. The next thirty seconds were full of frantic action. The big rattler was doing his best to strike me and sink those big fangs in my leg, and I was doing my best to thrash him with a mostly ineffective weapon. Somehow I beat that snake to death with my puny stick and got back out of the check before the rush of water arrived, but I'll never forget the fear with which I accomplished that feat. The yardstick didn't survive.

Another snake story took place on the ranch of Jason Horn, who happened to be the biggest cattle feeder in our valley. Horn paid for a lot of water, and I had to set many gates every time we made a run there. I was knee deep in the flow setting a gate when I looked up and saw one of Horn's Mexican field hands leaning on his shovel, and staring down at me from the top of the ditch. I tried to communicate with him using my limited high school Spanish. This fellow seemed to be friendly, so we continued our fragmented communication for several minutes.

He was standing on a on a twelve foot long, twelve inch wide, plank which lay on top of the bank. Coiled beneath it in a small hollow in the bank was a big green and brown prairie rattler. I was staring directly into the snake's eyes from about ten feet away. I shouted "rattler" at him, but he just stared and didn't seem to understand. I said, "rattle, rattle, buzz, buzz" and pointed to the hollow with my shovel. He got the message and leaped backward. Then he pulled the plank toward him with his shovel and exposed the snake. He let go a stream of Spanish expletives, and the shovel flashed through the air two hundred times in the next thirty seconds, and consequently made mince meat of the reptile. The whole scene was so preposterous! I was laughing so hard I nearly fell over and drowned in the rushing water.

As I have mentioned before, water was life-blood to these folks of the prairie. How precious the farmers believed it to be was made clear to me as I brought in a water run at four a.m. one morning shortly before I retired from this work forever. I was setting a gate about fifty feet away from a dark farmhouse. Evidently the farmer who lived there thought that I was a water thief (sometimes neighbors stole water from each other). Whack! whack! Two rifle shots slammed into the water beside me and burrowed into the bank I was leaning against. I am not a dumb fellow, and so I was in the coupe and down the road in record time. I didn't stop shaking for about an hour. Well, that's a little taste of my great summer job. I wouldn't have missed it for all the water or snakes in Louisiana.

15. WINTER MIRACLE

Cruncher Carson, Whitey Stoneacre, and I picked our way carefully down the sagebrush covered wash that cut into the bluffs above the Bijou River one cold November morning. In the Spring of every year a mighty river rolled down this old riverbed, tossing and rolling like the Columbia for about a month, and then it became just a stream running through the great gulch cut by the Spring activity. There were about five inches of snow on the ground that day. It crackled with each step we took, and that sound somehow added to the joy of our hunt. We were looking for pheasants, but we wouldn't turn down a shot at a healthy jack rabbit either.

Pheasant and rabbit were staples of our winter diet. All of us were public school teachers, and badly needed to supplement our family's food supply as the teacher salaries of the fifties were pathetically low. The mostly dry bed of the winter Bijou had a great many game birds and animals living near its meager stream and sloughs, but it was pheasant season, and that was our objective on this particular hunting day. In addition to the topography, what made the Bijou bottoms very special were the people who lived and worked on the bluffs above cut by the half-mile wide riverbed. These were people who somehow managed to survive on land that was probably too poor even for the government to grant to an Indian tribe.

Whitey Stoneacre and his family lived seven miles west of Ft. Darwin on the bluffs creating the north side of the Bijou. Whitey and his wife, Sadie, had three tow-headed little girls. All five of them worked many hours every day bringing Bijou number two-reservoir water to their acre plot of vegetables. Whitey was a Voc-Ag teacher at Darwin High School, and somehow he and his wife had found enough money to build a house on the wasteland on the top of the bluff. They made it a little spot of paradise in a vast, desolate prairie. It was a place where five very nice people welcomed the sun every morning, and then did their damndest to make their existence on the prairie count for something. Whitey was a small, athletic man who hunted many times with Cruncher and I. He was very quick, and could run for miles.

Quite often, when we hunted Canada geese, he would sprint under a circling flock and be in a trench with his shotgun uplifted as the beautiful birds set their wings to sail into a field. He was so quiet that he frequently would scare the be-jibbers out of you by sneaking up from behind, and then saying something to you when you thought that he must be miles away. At other times when we were hunting, the three of us would split up in order to cover more ground, and after what seemed like hours of tramping, I would spot a lone tree in the prairie, and head for it to rest for a few moments in its cool shade. Just when I had leaned against the tree to relax a while, and just as I had lit my old pipe with contentment, Whitey, without a sound, would materialize from the other side of that same tree. I swear to God, his sudden appearance was many times more startling than running into a range bull. Naturally, we called Whitey "the Indian."

Another family that we all knew well, the Wilkersons, lived across from Whitey on the south side of the Bijou. Old Sam Wilkerson managed to grow about seventy acres of sugar beets every year in land that was a mixture of sand and rock. He also kept bees, and his apiary supplied honey to all of Platte County. I can remember driving into Sam's yard on many different occasions, and seeing him dressed in bee-keeper helmet and net, walking back toward his house with a large comb of fresh honey. The sight of him in this attire always startled me as I had heard many times that Sam was one of the last of the old mountain men who had somehow lived into my own time.

The Wilkerson's also kept a huge German Shepherd dog chained to the shed behind their house, whose job it was to discourage unwelcome visitors. The dog's name was Pal, but he was a friend only to Sam and his family. This dog always put on a show of pulling mightily at his chain, growling viciously, and baring his teeth at me when I drove into the yard. All the years I visited Sam for honey and conversation, I never came within twenty feet of Pal.

Back to the pheasant hunt. Cruncher,Whitey, and I had walked about two miles east on the Bijou bottom that day and had seen nothing but a very cold blue sky, miles of snow-covered prairie, and an incredible collection of frosted sage and mesquite. Then about 500 yards ahead, we saw, right in the middle of the riverbed, a single forty-foot cottonwood, which had somehow survived the annual spring floods that rolled down the Bijou. There was something strange about it. From a distance it appeared to be in full leaf in the dead of winter, and presented a startling black image against the snowfields, which lay behind it. We approached cautiously, and when we were about fifty feet away, we saw an incredible sight. Bright shimmering jewels of emerald green and royal purple seemed to flash out toward us as if they adorned the bright white, frost covered limbs of the tree.

The giant old cottonwood was not in leaf, but rather full of pheasants, probably about five hundred of them. That tree full of pheasants was astoundingly beautiful in the early morning sun light. All those beautiful birds were roosting within easy gun shot range. We had walked miles through the cold dawn for just such an opportunity, but now not one of us could raise a gun and pull the trigger. This startling image seemed almost to almost be some sort of incredibly beautiful religious revelation. They were just too damn beautiful to kill, and somehow, shooting at them now would have been a dastardly violation of their cottonwood sanctuary and of them, and, in a certain way, of God.

We watched them for a few minutes, and the pheasants, which now must have been aware of our presence, still remained sitting in close formation in their tree. We finally turned and started our long walk back to the car. No one said a word, but we all knew that, once again, our spirits had been renewed by the savage beauty of the Bijou Bottoms. The place seemed to take on a spiritual nature at the most unlikely of times. As we climbed the bluffs, and finally got back into the car our game-bags empty, I realized that sometimes spiritual contentment is more fulfilling than a full belly, and also that on many occasions, you can encounter the damndest things out on the prairie.

16. THE GREAT RAMJET

He waited silently in the darkness cut by the sun behind a great concrete pillar. Every muscle in his body was tensed for the attack. His heart hammered with excitement and anticipation. He knew that if he just had patience, she would be coming along. Finally, he heard her. Thump, thump, swish, thump, thump, swish, her footsteps sounded as she made her way toward that concrete pillar behind which he was hiding. Then he glimpsed her white face. He leaped from behind the pillar and caught her by the shoulders. Now he would have his way with her.

I think that we should take a break from the history of the Hawke family, and I will tell you the story of a remarkable rabbit. Roger Ramjet was a western jackrabbit. I understand that jackrabbits really are hares, but in Platte county, if you talked about a Jackhare, no one would know what in Archie's barn you were talking about. Roger had a black spot at the end of his tail, an incredibly developed libido, and great springs in his mighty back legs.

This is a story about how this incredible rabbit got a high school education, and entered, for a time, what must have been paradise on earth for him. In rabbit history, he must be an esteemed character of legend not unlike James Bond had become in the area of female conquest. The only difference is that everything I'm going to tell you about Ramjet is absolutely true. This ain't no novel. I was there, and I witnessed this character in action many times.

One Easter. Swifty Fasbacher, head football coach at Ft. Darwin High School, in a moment of profound tenderness or weakness, decided that he would buy two very white, very sweet, little female bunnies for his two pre-school daughters. It was grand idea until Swifty's wife, Sarah, said that she could not stand one more day of vacuuming rabbit raisins off their good carpet. The damn things got sticky when the furnace came on, and their basset hound ground them into the rug. Those messy bunnies had to find a new home.

The year before that, Ft. Darwin had built a new high school. It was built in a raised octagon shape around an open court-yard. The school library connected to both sides of the octagon in the inner courtyard by wide, elevated halls, sat in the middle of a complex of classrooms running around the octagon. It was the sort of a building that architects and school boards dream about - showy, expensive, and totally inefficient. A beautiful lawn was cultured in the enclosed courtyard. Our building administrators decided that the lawn was for students and visitors to look at, but not to walk on.

Swifty thought that this grassy paradise was a perfect place to release the Easter rabbits. His daughters would approve of his plan, and he knew that the high school students would just love to watch the antics of the bunnies. Swifty pointed out that perpetually difficult students (those in our recalcitrant file) could be selected to water and feed the little females daily, thereby removing those trouble-makers from the classroom for a few minutes on a regular basis, and consequently, giving both rabbits and teachers a badly needed break.

If the school principal, Dr. Seldom Wright, would just agree to Swifty's plan, the coach's rabbit problem would be solved. Eager for local attention for any reason, Dr. Wright did agree, and the two female rabbits were released to graze on the beautiful grass. Just as Swifty had envisioned, the students were fascinated with this addition to their school, and many stood on outside balconies built inside the octagon (when they should have been in class) to watch the rabbits as they ate and romped contentedly. This was education for life.

It was at this point that the real adventure began. A tall, lanky ranch boy named Walt Wayne, all-state half-back no less, got the bright idea that an additional rabbit might really spice things up. So he captured a male jackrabbit with a great black spot on his pointy tail on his father's cattle ranch north of Ft. Darwin. One cool night in the fall of that year, Walt and his buddies scaled the walls of the courtyard and released the jack rabbit, soon to be known as Roger Ramjet, into what would become a great experience for this big fella.

The teachers were stunned by this event, so the principal called an unusual evening faculty meeting. Billie Montrose, an aging but respected biology teacher whose main claims to fame were the dozens of rattlesnakes she had pickled in gallon jars around her room rose to speak and said, "Not to worry, wild rabbits will never mate with domestic rabbits."

The principal and faculty, thus reassured by this voice of great education and wisdom, adjourned the meeting with a definite sense of relief. Somewhere out in the dark courtyard, Roger must have put up a mighty cheer. Within days of the faculty decision, crowds of students, many with their teachers as guides and interpreters, appeared daily on those **balconies** surrounding the courtyard. Roger watching got so popular that an instructor had to reserve space if he or she really wanted a class to see the action clearly. Roger was an absolutely amazing performer. He would wait quietly behind a wall until the two female bunnies approached. Then he would fly out at them causing the white, fuzzy girls to leap into the air in a state of total disarray. Roger was an amazing athlete. He would catch the girl bunnies in mid-flight and then couple with them before they hit the ground. The crowds on the balconies would roar and cheer. Soon people were coming from miles around to see this incredible jackrabbit. The county news paper,The Ft. Darwin Drum, sent a reporter out to write a piece, and Dr. Seldom Wright reveled in this new found fame.

After a few months of this incredible show, the courtyard was full of new bunnies. The biology teacher said it defied biological logic, and was obviously some sort of miracle. By Christmas of the following year there were hundreds of rabbits - white, brown, and brown-white - roaming in herds around the courtyard. The student council appointed special students-of-the-month to direct the watering and feeding of the ever increasing rabbit population, and the recalcitrant trouble-makers were thereby reduced to the status of subservient soldiers in the cause of servicing our rabbit herd.

Soon the rabbits began to realize the need for organized warrens, and began tunneling under the great octagon shaped high school building. They also tunneled under the pylons holding up the library in the middle of the courtyard. About the fifteenth of May, just a little more than two years after the two white bunnies and Roger had been introduced to the courtyard, the library collapsed with a great roar and a cloud of dust into a multitude of tunnels dug by the rabbits. There was a great crash and giant cloud of dust. A huge crack appeared in the courtyard walls, and then the courtyard walls completely burst asunder. Hundreds of survivor rabbits leaped through the breach and ran down a long hill toward the South Platte River and its forest and bushes a half-mile to the north. Some say they were led in this rabbit stampede to safety and freedom by a jackrabbit with a black spot at the end of his tail who made amazing leaps down the hillside toward the river bottom.

Within hours, the rabbits had all disappeared from Ft. Darwin High School. The school board immediately had to get ready for a bond issue election, the proceeds of which to be used for the necessary repairs on the new school, which had suddenly collapsed into a rabbit hole. Swifty Fasbacher took a job in a school four hundred miles away, and Dr. Seldom Wright and Billie Montrose never again, at any time or on any occasion mentioned rabbits or hares.

The legend, however, of Roger Ramjet, father of his people and high school graduate, is still noised throughout Platte County, and Swifty Fasbacher is still revered as the one teacher who brought genuine excitement and real knowledge to the students of this prairie school.

17. WAUGH DAY

Financial survival wasn't easy for a teacher's family in Ft. Darwin around the middle of the twentieth century. Summer Meadow, my wife, worked for The Chamber of Commerce, the Federal Land Bank, the Provident Finance Company, the Rancher's State Bank, and as a child care provider in our home in an attempt to make my meager teaching salary stretch far enough to maintain a young family. I taught five classes during the regular year, coached two sports, ran the school district's audio-visual division, worked for the Bijou Irrigation company as a ditch- rider, worked for Safeway as a piss-ant for all seasons, and taught summer school and night school every time either program was offered to the community.

Summer knew that this couldn't go on forever as Spring and Sage, our two young children, were growing up and deserved a chance to go to college.

So somehow she found time to commute to Colorado State College in Greeley to start taking college classes in an attempt to get her own teaching certificate. We thought that perhaps two teaching salaries could bring about the family's financial survival. But that's another part of the story; let's go back to Ft. Darwin and Waugh Day.

Times were difficult for all prairie folks, and just about everybody else in this town also worked at many different jobs in their own attempt to make it. In the middle of their frenzy of activity came the annual community celebration known as "Waugh" Day. Every August the people of Ft. Darwin quit working for a day, put on their new levis or print dresses, let their hair down, and had a parade, programs at the city swimming pool and town square park, and a genuine carnival at night.

"Waugh" is an expression known only in the West. In the old days trappers and mountain men who worked the Platte River would, in their moments of greatest happiness or achievement, throw their head back and shout "Waugh". No one knew what this actually meant, but it seemed an appropriate expression, both for the mountain men, and for those citizens of Ft. Darwin in their annual celebration which, thereforth, became known as"Waugh" Day.

It was just such a "Waugh Day' in l960 that marked our son Sage's debut on the community stage. Sage was really Sage Mountain Hawke, but at four years of age, he was such a serious, determined little fellow that when he got the requisite crew cut of that time, it just seemed right that his moniker should be "Toughy". His big sister, the princess Spring, who was really Summer's and Rock's oldest child, had been a participant for two years in the "Waugh Day" parade dressed in her ballet costume and riding her half-pint bike just in front of the new International tractors and the Ft. Darwin fire truck. Toughy had and watched and waited, and this year was his chance. Summer dressed him in a teddy-bear costume and turned him loose. The day had gone well. The parade had moved down the two-block business district known as Main Street; two teen-age boys had climbed a greased telephone pole and captured the pig tied to the top; many races had been swum in the swimming pool; pies, cakes, and quilts had been on appropriate display, and then came the high-light of the day in the town square. Slim Peabody, a Denver television personality, was hosting a talent show in the community band shell. Summer and Spring were in the crowd watching their young neighbors display great talent of many kinds when Summer noticed that Toughy wasn't with them. Not to worry. After all this was Ft. Darwin and it was 1960.

The entertainment had gone on for about an hour when suddenly Slim Peabody stopped the program and came toward the middle of the stage leading a two-and-a-half foot teddy bear by the hand. The crowd cheered. Slim said, "It seems that I have found a teddy bear who has lost his mother. This little bear is mad as a wet hen, and says he wants his mother. If she is present, will she come forward and claim her bear?" Summer hurried to get our child.

Toughy would later that same year wander off from his family when we were on vacation, find that he was lost again, this time in a strange town and in a very strange park. He demonstrated his maturity by finding a phone booth and trying to call home. He was learning how to handle a crisis. His problems were now two - naturally there was no one at home, and, to make matters worse, he couldn't get out of the damn phone booth. This incident was many years before Steven Spielberg had E.T. "call home" in a movie that certainly affected the lives of millions of children. Sage was always way ahead of his time.

Eventually this lad became a supervising attorney working for the fifth Circuit Court of Appeals, and then lawyer and legislative counsel helping to form new governments in the muti-islanded country of Micronesia in the south Pacific, which I guess, demonstrates that early signs of greatness are sometimes difficult to read. Now he has two little bears of his own who, undoubtedly, will demonstrate the excellence of their Hawke genes when they find themselves in similar situations.

Waugh Day always concluded with a carnival and street dance. It is difficult to know how many new Ft. Darwin families were begun at the time of our annual celebration, but this great day certainly played a part in the growth of our community. Waugh! Waugh! Waugh!

18. MIDNIGHT MEETING

(or, you haven't come a long way yet, baby)

Garvey Barnes had been the best known labor organizer in Colorado for twenty years. He was headquartered in the big steel town in the southern part of the state. Garvey was a formidable man who looked the part of a life-time union boss. As local president of the teacher's organization, I thought he was just the man to represent us in our first annual negotiation with the school board. This opportunity for negotiation was something I had finally managed to get started during my tenure as leader of our local teacher's organization. I wanted very much for it to succeed.

In previous years individual teachers had had to plead their case for a raise before an individual board member. Usually we asked for something stupendous like a $100 annual raise. After my first year of teaching, I remember very well walking through an acre of spring mud to run down such a board member who was busy disking his fields on the seat of an old International tractor, and then begging for an extra hundred for the following year. That year I didn't get the raise.

In the following two years I experienced some prosperity. My salary had risen to the grand sum of more than four thousand dollars. Finally now (1961), for the first time in history, the teacher's elected representative was allowed to come before the board and plead for an increase for all the teachers at once for the following contract year. I was that representative. It was my third year in the district, and I was working sixty-five hours a week at Ft. Darwin High. I was paid a base salary of 3,450 dollars (six daily classes), plus150 dollars for coaching three sports (450), and another 150 bucks for running the Audio-visual program in the twelve schools of the district, 600 more bucks for running the Debate club and the intra-mural program, and 180 bucks for teaching summer school six hours a day for ten weeks, but the grand total of 4830 dollars still didn't begin to support my young family of four. I still had to borrow 100 dollars a month just to pay for groceries. In other words, teachers were paid as little as possible for being entrusted with the community's most precious possession, its young.

Then I found a great idea. Teachers shouldn't have to beg for an annual increase. They should be paid a base salary, which would allow them to pay for rent and groceries. There should be a salary schedule guaranteeing annual raises. The schedule should be based on education and experience. Such a plan might get a classroom teacher to $10,000 dollars a year, if he or she had taught at Fort Darwin for twenty years and had earned a master's degree in the interim.

What finally happened was that Ft. Darwin became one of the first school districts in the state to have an incremental salary schedule. However, there was a price to be paid first.

One night at midnight, my personal witching hour in this case, I had returned home from the board meeting at which I had acted as the teacher's representative in salary talks for the following contract year. I had talked Garvey Barnes into making the two hundred-mile trips from his labor headquarters and appearing with me in front of the board. The board members had appeared to be in a state of shock when I introduced a real labor man to them. Garvey said a few words about the importance of organizing teachers, and paying them a living wage, and then he sat down.

The board listened carefully to my proposal for a guaranteed salary step schedule, based on experience and education, but were totally non-committal about what that salary schedule should be when Garvey and I had been excused from the meeting at about eleven o'clock.

I bought Garvey a quick cup of coffee, gave him many heart-felt thanks for his trip and appearance (all

I could afford), and headed for home as I had to be in school the next morning at 7:15. I had just jumped into bed when the phone rang. It was Randall O'Neill, the board president, and he wanted me to return immediately to the board meeting across town.

When I walked in at midnight, it was obvious that the fat was in the fire. The board and the superintendent were scowling as I sat down. First I got a twenty minute lecture on the great insult I had given them as, obviously, I had forgotten the love and responsibility that the board felt for the teaching staff (it took several more years to get rid of this paternalistic attitude on he part of the board). I heard that they had always taken care of their teachers and would continue to in the future, and that they resented the fact that I had brought an outsider into our negotiations, particularly a labor organizer who was probably a communist as well. Then the ax fell. Dr. Charles Clock, our esteemed leader, the superintendent of schools in Platte County, known to his loyal staff as Ol' Doc Ding-Dong, rose from his chair, faced me, and then began my sentence for insubordination. "Rock, we are all deeply disappointed in you. Your proposal has threatened to end a mutually respectful relationship between administration and staff. We therefor feel that a punishment for this indiscretion is necessary."

I could feel the wrath of my elders and betters cutting into my very being. My God, what had I done to the relative security of my family? The great doctor of education continued, "We therefore are terminating all your extra-curricular assignments as of this minute." With one slash of their furious pen, they had deprived me of about 100 bucks a month. Feeling completely helpless and betrayed, I decided on he spot that I had had a belly-full of this chicken outfit, and that I must find somewhere else to teach. We didn't leave Ft. Darwin, however, for six more years. I really didn't have the courage to do what needed to be done, and the under-class hadn't become empowered quite yet.

19. HOW'S THAT?

Jack Wayne was a short, tough little rancher who favored black cowboy hats and very large gold belt buckles. His neighbors claimed that he had been a champion bronc rider in his youth. Jack and his family lived eighteen miles north of Ft. Darwin, which meant that his thousand-acre ranch lay as close to Wyoming as it did to Darwin. The very steep-sided Wildcat Gulch ran through his property, but most of his ranch was rolling prairie. This whole area had been used as a hunting ground by the Southern Cheyenne who held an untold number of buffalo runs near the Wildcat gulch for perhaps a thousand years before the pioneers arrived. Jack managed a huge herd of twenty-five hundred head of Hereford and Angus cows near a range of mesas generally known as The Cheyenne Buttes. These high buttes thrust their rocky heads high in the sky just south of the Wyoming border.

Jack was the genuine article as far as to him being an old time cattleman and rancher was concerned. He was honest, sincere, and nearly inarticulate. That is to say, he rarely said much to anybody. Jack had a tall, muscular son named Walt who was one hell of a halfback for the Ft. Darwin Indians football team. The boy probably got his size from his six-foot Scandinavian mother. Walt was accorded all-state honors as a high school junior, and when the local high school team qualified for the state championship during his senior year, naturally the community of Ft. Darwin had to have a grand community pep rally before the football boys boarded the old yellow school bus to ride to the championship game in Denver.

Dr. Seldom Wright, the High school principal, was put in charge of organizing the event. The organization of such a major event was proving to be more than he could comprehend. However, he got what seemed to be a huge break when he was surprised two days before the rally by the figure of Jack Wayne appearing in his office doorway

"Howdy Mister," said Jack.

"Well, come right in," said Dr. Wright.

Jack rubbed his huge hands together, then he rubbed his belt buckle and began to speak "I'm a proud bastard," he said

Dr. Wright, not used to this rough language, never-the-less regained his composure and answered, "With very good reason, Jack."

"I want to speak to those boys at the rally," announced Jack.

Dr. Wright sat up straight in his chair as visions of newspaper pictures and stories swam through his mind. He smiled and said, "What a wonderful suggestion, Jack. Of course I'll have to clear it with the

Superintendent and the school board, but I feel certain they will be receptive. The rally will be in our gym on Thursday at 10 o'clock. I'll look forward to seeing you a little before ten that morning."

"Right." said Jack.

The great day arrived, and Ft. Darwin had turned out in all its magnificence for the rally. The high school student body, the Superintendent and the school board, the ministerial alliance, the editor of the newspaper and all his reporters, the owner of the radio station with a direct on-the-air line ready to go, the complete roster of the Chamber of Commerce, all the members of the Platte County Medical Association (doctors and dentists and nurses galore), the manager of the local Sugar beet factory and all his workers (the plant was closed for the occasion), the Parent-Teacher Association, all the members of the Farmer-Rancher Co-op and their wives, the faculty and staff of all the schools in Ft. Darwin the twelve piece Mesquite pep band led by band director Errol Flynn McGraw, and, of course, all the proud parents of the boys on the football team were there. Every soul who truly counted for miles around, except, of course, for all the unfortunate mothers with small children, was there, all on their very best behavior and wearing clothes that they hoped were most appropriate for this earth-stopping occasion. Probably nothing of this magnitude had ever happened in Ft. Darwin before.

The rally began with the Indian fight song "Fight on, you Ft. Darwin Red Men" echoing and re-echoing throughout the cavernous gymnasium. Twelve very pretty high school cheer leaders dressed in short Pochahontas costumes danced and pranced through their series of chants, and then Dr. Ben Clock, District School Superintendent (known as ding-Dong to the faculty and staff) stood up as a man who was clearly a legend in his own mind, and approached the microphone.

"We are gathered here today to celebrate one of the grandest accomplishments to come about during my term as administrator of this school district," pronounced Ben. Next there was a short silence as the Super tried to organize his well-educated thoughts.

He continued, "I want to introduce Dr. Wesley Majors, pastor of our Methodist church and head of the ministerial alliance who has an appropriate prayer." Thunderous applause exploded up and down both sides of the basketball court, and then the audience obediently bowed their heads.

"Let us pray," said the minister, and two thousand heads snapped into an even more appropriate posture of supplication. "We ask our Lord to protect each and every member of this football team and their coaches. We further ask that a marvelous VICTORY be won for Ft. Darwin. Amen." There ensued a respectful religious silence, and then a tremendous roar, which should have been heard by the cows on Jack Wayne's ranch. The great noise of prospective victory shook the structure.

Next Dr. Seldom Wright came before the throng. "In the words of one of the fathers of this wonderful team of ours, I am so proud! So proud! I have here another man who told me of his own great pride in this splendid team a couple of days ago. I want to introduce Jack Wayne, father of our all-state halfback, Walt Wayne."

Again there was a thunderstorm of frantic applause, and now tears had begun to flow from some members of the audience. Sherry Bratmealer, the school librarian, was having a great deal of trouble controlling herself. It was clearly a most significant day in the history of our town.

Jack Wayne, bronc-buster and cattle-rancher, walked slowly to the podium. He rubbed those hands together, and then they went to his rodeo belt buckle. For a few seconds he didn't say anything, and then he said, "Waugh!" The crowd went wild. Our Head football coach "Swifty" Fasbacher and I were sitting in the front row of bleachers six feet from Jack, and we could see his obvious emotion. Swifty was greatly enjoying the experience, and, I'm sure, regarded the possible state championship as the almost achieved pinnacle of his long and difficult career.

The old cowboy continued, although it was apparent that his feelings were about to get the best of him. "I love these boys, he said. "I want them to go out there on Saturday, ….. to go out there," he seemed here to struggle for just the right words, … "to go out there, go out there …and FART THEIR HITES OUT!!!." This last phrase re-echoed throughout the basketball arena. Old Jack, who suddenly realized what he had just shouted into the microphone, had the look of man who had just been struck dead by a thunder bolt.

There was no applause. There was not a sound from the audience, not even a single strangled giggle.

There was absolute silence for what seemed to be an eternity of time. The Ft. Darwin cheerleaders seemed to be frozen in place. Jack finally turned from the microphone, and quickly did a sort of bow-legged slide back toward his seat. Since the radio station had picked up this profound utterance, farmhouses throughout Northeastern Colorado were undoubtedly exploding with laughter. Swifty and I were pinching each other as hard as we could to keep from embarrassing ourselves, or this good man who had tried his damndest, and then screwed it up as badly as he possibly could have.

The principal didn't go on with his carefully planned program. He did not ask the head coach to speak. The pep band and cheerleaders did not reappear for an encore. There were no more words from civic leaders. The rally had been brought to an abrupt and unexpected end. The huge crowd just filed very quietly out of the gymnasium. What more could possibly be said or done? Well, that's the story of Jack Wayne and the Pep Rally. The football team and its followers greatly enjoyed the trip to the championship game. Everybody probably had a good meal in a big restaurant. The game was played on a cold November day on frozen ground in a really big stadium. The opponent was a parochial school team from the Denver league. Walt Wayne ran for 147 total yards in a losing cause. The rural lads tried mightily, but they were overwhelmed by the sophistication of the larger school. The final score was Immaculate Conception 21, Ft. Darwin 14.

When I think back on that incident after all these years, I am reminded of the great differences between prairie folk and their urban counterparts. No one in that throng at that incredibly humorous moment in time wanted to further humiliates that old rancher. Furthermore, I will always remember a proud old cowboy, and what must have been one of the grandest faux pas in the history of the Colorado prairie.

20. IT'S YOU, ROCK!

There were about a thousand people in the auditorium that Spring in 1963 when I came in one of the back doors to take my place in the audience for disciplinary control. The general assembly that day promised to be one of the better assemblies of the year, and was much anticipated by students and staff alike as the program was billed as the awarding of the yearbook's dedication to the "teacher of the year." This was always a happy time for someone on the staff and, in addition, the assembly always got the teaching staff positive mention in the local community newspaper. For the students, it was also an activity that meant that the school year was close to the end and they would soon be free for a few months.

That spring had been difficult for me, and I hadn't thought about which one of our venerable old-timers would receive the accolades of the annual staff.

Claude M. Higgins, Jr.

I settled in my seat on the aisle and set about checking out which troublemakers were seated near me. I had been at Ft. Darwin High School for five years or so and finally felt as if I had become a member of its faculty, and to some extent, I had begun to understand its traditions and politics of our little world. There was a cadre of respected old-time staff members who had been there since the invention of dirt. There were younger, flashier, administrative types who had the eye of the county education office, and then there were the rest of us. I felt as if I had just recently qualified for "the rest of us." Each previous spring I had waited for the dreaded call to the principal's office where he would tell me I had better apply somewhere else or, hopefully, that I could look forward to another year of hard work and low pay. On that particular day the students were a little noisier and more boisterous than usual as the principal arose from his chair on the stage and introduced the student editor of the yearbook.

Judy, this year's yearbook editor, was a cute blonde who had struggled through first period English with me. She pulled the microphone closer to her and said, "The annual staff has decided that the 1963 yearbook should be dedicated to a relatively new member of our teaching faculty. Rock Hawke, would you please come forward?"

Behind me I heard Kangaroo Carby, our social studies teacher and track coach, say, "Get up there, Rock."

In total shock and amazement I made my way down the main aisle and walked toward the stage. The kids in the student body were on their feet applauding, and as I approached the stage, I could see Summer, my wife, waiting near the podium. In front of the stage microphone I was, indeed, speechless. How could this happen to someone on the very bottom of the totem pole? I don't remember what I mumbled in appreciation of this honor, but it was probably something inane and inappropriate. I do remember hugging my wife and having a great lump in my throat as I left the spotlight. I discovered later that Summer had known about this award for some time, and had provided pictures of our young family for publication in that year's yearbook.

This incident of recognition and acknowledgment was to forever change my attitude about teaching. For the first time, I had an identity in my chosen profession, and I had received an honor that was going to force me to try to live up to the fact of being acknowledged as a good teacher. Every teacher needs such a renewal of the idealism, which they must have had in order to enter this crazy business in the first place. But for this to happen to Rock Hawke! Incredible! Waugh again!

21. ALWAYS A BRIDESMAID

One of the high points in my golf-coaching career also turned out to be one of my greatest disappointments. This was to be our year as far as my high school golf team was concerned. We had been bridesmaids three times in the past, and now were ready to grab the golden ring for ourselves. I had coached golf in Fort Darwin for eight years before that spring in l965, and we had had good teams in the past, but this year was different. We had been undefeated during this particular season, and then had won both the conference and district golf tournaments. We were a perfect 31 and 0 going into Colorado Springs to play for the state championship.

That year my team was led by two seniors, Mark McBride, and Paul Remington. Mark and Paul had both averaged about 68.5 strokes a round during the season. My number there and four men were

Paul's younger brothers, Ken, a junior, and Bobby, a sophomore. They both had high seventy averages. In other words, it was a darn good high school team. The Remington family was very interesting. The mother of my three golfing brothers had been the chef at the country club for years. Her cabbage pockets were so famous that visiting coaches invariably took a couple dozen home with them every time they visited Darwin. The father of this family had an equally long career as the groundskeeper for the course, so the three boys had grown up there. It showed. All three were excellent golfers, and all three later became professional golfers in their adult life.

My number one man, Mark, could easily have become a successful golfer on the professional's tour. I saw him beat Hale Irwin twice in playoffs for tournament medallist his senior year. Instead of turning pro, Mark later took over his father's business, married a local girl and raised a family. He remained the outstanding amateur golfer in the state for many years, but unfortunately, the nation never had the opportunity to see in a professional playoff with the great Irwin.

Well, here I was with this outstanding team. We were ready, and then on the first day of the tournament, Colorado was struck with a freak snowstorm. About six inches fell the night before the tournament, but on the morning of the tournament dawned clear and cold. The officials decided that the championship would go on even though the temperature was a good thirty degrees colder than any match we had played previously that spring. My number one was particularly affected. He started shaking on the first tee, and his hands just wouldn't be still. I drove down town and brought gloves for the boys, but it didn't work for Mark. He shot an eighty. The Remington boys held it together, and all scored in the low and mid-seventies. As a result, we were one shot ahead of Longmont, a team that we had beaten three times already during the regular season, at the end of the first day's play in the state tournament.

The second day of this two-day tournament came on as clear, but still cold. Mark had a better day and shot a seventy-two. The Remington boys played their hearts out, each of them improving on his first day's performance by a shot or two. We ended this thing with a highly respectable score, which would have won in eight of the previous ten-year's tournaments, but this year it wasn't good enough. The Longmont team played better than they ever had before. Their number 3 and 4 players both shot 69. We lost the team championship by two strokes. The best laid plans, etc… Even with this bitter defeat I was, and remain to this day, extremely proud of this team. These four boys were fine young fellows who grew up to be fine men. After some serious soul searching at the tournament's end, we celebrated the fact of our participation, and that we came damn close. Close not only to the championship, but also close to each other.

That is what high school athletics are really about anyway, but that first place trophy would have looked awfully nice in our trophy case back in Darwin.

22. THE KEY INCIDENT

One cold, snowy Monday morning an announcement came over Ft. Darwin High School's inter-com at 7:05. Such interruptions of our planning time before class each day was common. This announcement was ominously different.

A harsh voice ordered, "All male teachers come immediately to the student center."

I made my way from the English office through the maze of halls toward the nerve center of our building. An early morning storm I had driven through to get to school had passed, the winter sun was out, and the student center in our shinning new school was sunny and almost overwhelmingly bright with well-polished chrome and tile. It had been a restful and welcome weekend, and I was getting psyched up to face two hundred kids in the next eight hours. I really resented this damned squawk box interruption. It seemed as if there had been a lot more about the administration of our school that I resented lately.

The thirty-six male teachers on the staff soon assembled in the student center that fateful morning, and programmed by many years in the public school system, we lined up to face our stern -looking principal. Dr. Kramer Haug had been principal at Ft. Darwin for four years, and had established a less-than-friendly relationship with his staff. He was fifty, over-stuffed, and belligerent. As a staff we had talked privately about what seemed to be a trend toward autocratic decision-making on the part of our fearless leader.

Without any pleasantries, he began. "Our Voc-Ag shop was robbed over the week-end. About four thousand dollars worth of tools were taken. There was no forced entry. Someone with a key robbed us. Take out your keys."

Swifty Fasbacher, our football coach who was standing next to me, mumbled. "What the hell is the Old Man up to?"

"Damned if I know," was my intelligent reply.

"No talking," barked Haug All up and down the line of teachers looks were shot back and forth which indicated that what ever this was, we were just about through taking this kind of nonsense..

"Now that's a pleasant way to start our day," said Cruncher Carson, standing on my other side. Cruncher had a deep commanding sort of voice that rumbled across the polished floor and off our new tile walls. Haug ignored this remark as Cruncher had been a professional football player in the thirties, a professional wrestler in the forties, and still looked as if he could go bear hunting with a switch.

The principal turned to his vice-principal, Wilfred Carby, and said, "Check "em."

Carby was a tall, bald junior administrator who always appeared to be on the verge of a nervous breakdown. He was the Athletic Director of our school, and also had the "awesome" responsibility of maintaining and checking out keys to personnel. Now in his fifties, and aware of the fact that he was now too old to get a job in most school districts, Wilfred didn't want to do anything to screw up his retirement. Therefore, he swallowed a lot of pride on a daily basis, and jumped when the big man growled.

Wilfred made his way down the line looking carefully at the ring of keys each of us extended toward him. I couldn't believe or understand what was happening. In retrospect, I have often regretted my not thinking of the right thing to do at that particular moment in time. One or all of us should have challenged the old autocrat immediately instead of obeying his insulting command.

"What the hell would looking at our keys prove?" asked Cruncher.

Haug didn't acknowledge the question, but just turned and made his way up the staircase toward his office. We put our keys away and stood for a moment staring at each other in disbelief at what at just happened.

"I guess that you're dismissed," said Wilfred.

At 3:45 that afternoon, our school day over, almost all of the male teachers met at the Ft. Darwin Bar and Grill to discuss the strange activities of that morning. A definite surliness and, in some cases, downright anger, was evident on our faces and in our body language as we took over our usual table and drew up our usual chairs. Our hot coffee finally arrived and the meeting began.

"That stupid son-of-a bitch. I felt like smashing him in the face," said Cruncher.

"I know what you mean. I'm really pissed," I said, hoping to add to Cruncher's feelings of betrayal.

"Rock, You were born pissed-off," said Elk Eberhart, the boy's P.E. instructor. I glared at him, but knew in the back of my mind that he was probably right. My usual attitude had, unfortunately, been one of anger in recent months.

For the next thirty minutes we cussed and discussed the key incident. Whitey Binford, our Voc. Ag. Teacher, a naturally quiet man if there ever was one, finally said, "This is horse shit. He insulted every one of us. I've had it with this kind of crap. I'm out of here."

"You're absolutely right," said Pudge Mounds our basketball coach. "It's time that we get out of Ft. Darwin." Looks of approval and the assertive nodding of many heads made their way around the table. Then a realization of the seriousness of our decision hit us all. In stunned silence we sat thinking about what Whitey and Pudge had said. We averaged about ten years experience apiece at Ft. Darwin High. How does one leave a relatively safe, tenured job? There were such things as security for one's family. Did we have the guts to cut ourselves adrift, put our families in deeper financial jeopardy, and go through the process of looking for another town and another job?

How the hell does one find a job that would offer you a position and a salary commensurate with what we had worked up to in the Ft. Darwin district? We thought about our wives' involvement in the community. What about our kids' positions in the school system? What about our extended families (many of us were from this area originally)?

At that moment the front door of the Grill opened, and in strolled Dr. Charles Clock, the Public School superintendent. A large, arrogant, pompous, man, he nodded to our assemblage and sat down at the bar for his afternoon treat of soft ice cream.

Jack Bose, social studies teacher, said "Maybe we should talk with Dr. Clock about this.

"Are you kidding?" said Cruncher. "Ding Dong needs help to zip up his pants in the morning."

That clinched it. Seven of us said almost in unison, "Whitey and Pudge are right. It's time to resign."
\

That's how nine male teachers left Darwin High School in one year. An incredibly stupid action by a high school principal helped us all make a decision that we probably should have made years earlier. We were off, for better or worse, to conquer new worlds. But what would we tell our wives? Well, let's see. In my own case, Summer, my wife, has always wanted to finish her education. We did need to have two teaching salaries if there is to be any chance to send our children to college. Things work out. We probably should have done this five years ago. We needed to find a good college town where Summer could go to school, and a town where there were more cultural opportunities for the family. Old Haug's stupidity made me think about my real responsibilities. What a good old bastard Haug really was. Windy Gap, here we come!

PART THREE
TEACHING IN WINDY GAP

Claude M. Higgins, Jr.

INTRODUCTION TO PART THREE

My last twenty-three years in the classroom were in another Colorado town, Windy Gap, ninety miles west of Ft. Darwin. It's earliest white invaders were searching for gold, and, as in the Ft. Darwin area, that meant that the Arapahoe and Cheyenne people had to be pushed out or exterminated. The miners, sodbusters, and cattlemen took Indian names for everything in sight, even built statues of their red brothers and extolled their virtues, but evidently decided finally that the native people themselves had no place in their new civilization.. What was really important was to steal their land. So they killed them or sent them unto reservations on land that no white man could ever want for any reason.

Now back to a little more on the Gap. This town sits at the bottom of a great land bowl. The Colorado Rocky Mountains rise sharply around the West Side of the community, and tall, rounded mesas guard this town in the other three directions. From its earliest days this town has been known as a center of culture and liberal sophistication, or if you prefer, the town of intellectual snobs and liberal foolishness. Today it is the Silicon Valley of Colorado, and the home of a major state university. Like Ft. Darwin, it once had a great abundance of wildlife to hunt and kill. Foxes, ducks, and Canada geese, eagles, cougars, bears, and mule and white tail deer can still be found in the foothills to the West (Thank God that we didn't shoot them all). In this part of Colorado, however, man has more nearly conquered nature than out on the prairie near Ft. Darwin. Windy Gap and its surrounding area have become almost too civilized for my taste.

It was to the lush meadows of the Windy Gap land bowl that I moved my family from Ft. Darwin near the middle of the twentieth century. After my resignation from Ft. Darwin High School, we packed our 1950 Chevrolet and headed west. The first years here were very difficult as we were almost without funds, and in that state of genteel poverty, but we were trying very hard to raise our family, finish my wife's education, and, of course, to establish our children in new schools.

These goals many times seemed impossible to achieve. Stubbornness always prevails, however, and after about three years, we finally seemed to be on the right track. Summer Meadow, my wife's fictional name in this narrative, had finished her degree and was teaching in the elementary schools of the valley. Spring Beauty and Sage, the names of our son and daughter, both were progressing through the public schools and preparing for college. Summer and I were both to teach here for more than twenty years, and both children finished high school in Windy gap and went on to get college degrees - a teacher's certificate on Spring's part, and a Law degree for Sage.

183

The people of this semi-mountain community were certainly different in some ways from the prairie folk we had known and loved in Ft. Darwin. They were more socially sophisticated, more career-oriented, more affluent, more concerned with the accumulation of wealth and position, somewhat more articulate, but certainly less interested in family and tradition. They were also, for the most part, lovable and generous. More intelligent and sensitive than the prairie folk, they were not. In many cases, they were dumber and less practical than those denizens of the prairie we had grown to know and love.

The names of people in this retrospective are all bogus, but most of the stories and some of the place names are true, or as authentic as my memory has allowed them to be. This re-naming of characters was done as much to protect the guilty as well as the innocent. Most importantly, it was also done to protect me from lawsuits. There are a million stories on the naked prairie and nude mountains of Colorado. There is considerable truth in all of the tales, which follow, and, sometimes, an occasional small lie.

23 EXTRACURRICULAR ACTIVITIES

Nudity, knifings, adultery, motorcycles, hogs and big snakes - sounds like a modern PG. rated film or a TV series shown during the family hours on network television, right? No, these things were just another day in the shop where I worked for thirty-three years - The Public schools. During the quarter century that I taught high school in Windy Gap, I witnessed many different kinds of student and staff behavior. Some of it was comic and foolish; other incidents were vicious and, sometimes, tragic. I will arbitrarily break this section into two parts. The reason for this is that the attitudes and behavior of our student body dramatically changed when the school was moved about five miles - from one side of town to the other in 1972 .

The first part of this piece will cover student escapades at the little school on the reservoir east of town, and the second part will contain some of my memories from the big, new, award-winning, Windy Gap high school home built on a ridge to the south of our city.

The old Windy Gap High was built in 1960. It was surrounded by many open fields and a few homes. A great irrigation and recreation reservoir bordered the campus on the east. This particular location dictated not only a different kind of students (primarily rural), but a different kind of student behavior as well. I will begin with a gentle story that took place in and near my classroom which was located on the west side of our old building with it's great view of the Rocky Mountains. The room had a half a dozen large windows exposing the spectacular foothills just a little to the west. It was a beautiful view that was incredibly lighted by each morning's sunrise. I taught "The Bible as History and Literature" in that room every morning at seven a.m. for three years. Naturally this class became known as the "Sunrise Services."

Claude M. Higgins, Jr.

In the fall of 1969, I had a good group of kids, which happened to include four members of our state championship football team. These four lads were all-American in every sense; all were genuine student-athletes. One of them I had arbitrarily chosen as the future husband for my daughter, Spring. She, however, was never interested, but, back to my tale.

I now admit that part of my technique in teaching this class was more than a little pompous. I began each hour with seriousness and reverence that I felt was appropriate for the subject matter and for our magnificent view. I kept my voice relatively soft and low in an attempt to gain respectful attention from the class. In such a posture, one cold morning, I was progressing though the magnificent story of the "Exodus". A few gentle feminine titters arose from the back of the room, and I knew without looking up that it must have something to do with my four footballers who had been strangely absent a few minutes ago when I took the daily roll.

I then looked up and caught sight of a red balloon slowly floating upward outside the last window in the room. It was followed at fifteen-second intervals by a green balloon, then a yellow one, and finally a bright blue balloon. I went back to that corner of the room, looked out the window, and discovered the culprits huddling just below the outside sill. When they saw me, the biggest and toughest popped up and said "Good Morning, Mr. Hawke. We thought that this is a perfect morning to make a pilgrimage to the pancake house."

The class emitted several whoops of delight, but they were very restrained whoops so as not to alert the administration. We adjourned outside, piled in four waiting pick-ups, and proceeded to a breakfast Bible meeting. I always felt that the best way to handle teen-agers was to give them what they wanted when possible, but within perimeters which I had always firmly established long ahead of any situation. Perhaps it is not necessary to say that Moses plays well with pancakes, or anything else for that matter.

The second incident I want to relate involved <u>Playboy</u> magazine, which at that point in time was just then becoming popular in the land of the free. I have an old friend named Duke Simmons, who happened to be head basketball coach and an exemplary social studies teacher as well. It was in his classroom that this story came about.

Duke was very serious about his teaching, and tried to give a very important and serious lecture to every class he met. He had a habit of lecturing facing the class, and at the same time, waving his pointer at locations, which he knew by heart on a map hanging from a frame on the wall behind him. His colleagues in the department knew about this map practice, and one day, used that knowledge to sabotage that good old fellow. He was working hard in front of his U.S. History class, thundering at them, and slashing back at his map with the pointer in order to make a point when the class collapsed in laughter. He hadn't noticed the collection of male teachers watching him through a small window in his door, and turned around to look back at his map, which seemed to be the place where the attention of the class was directed. On the map was the nude picture of Miss May in all her fleshly glory and he had been slashing at her with his pointer for two minutes.

In great embarrassment and frustration, he turned and tried to tear the center-fold from his map of the United States. He miscalculated and grabbed the heavy frame holding his entire supply of maps. With a mighty crash, the map rack slammed to the floor, but Miss May drifted free and sailed seductively across the class to the back of the room.

The old Windy Gap high school was built in a huge brick square of classrooms. In the center of the box ran a hallway connecting the two sides of the square. Classrooms and intermittent lockers lined this entire structure on both sides of every hall. It really was a very usable design that included tiled floors and walls throughout for easy maintenance. The athletic facilities, the gym and some additional classrooms, were tacked on the south side of the box at the front of the square. The cafeteria, student lounge, and Home Ec department had been attached at a back corner of the square. This entire layout was surrounded by ten acres of football stadium, playing fields, tennis courts, and parking lots, and bordered by wide expanses of green fields and ancient cottonwoods.

This complex was built on a piece of land between a two-lane blacktop and a reservoir. There were great earthen dikes surrounding the lake, which made perfect spots for outdoor classrooms. I have often thought that of the four high schools that I have taught in, this one had by far the best design and the most beautiful and useful campus.

The building held about twelve hundred students very comfortably. Why the school board just didn't add to this building when it became necessary to have a larger school is something I never understood. Instead they spent millions of taxpayer dollars on a series of hexagons that seemed to slide unnaturally down a hillside in south Windy Gap. Any form of government will find a way to spend money if you give them a chance.

Well, anyway, now that you have a picture of the place, I want to tell you about the masked motorcycle rider. The locker and classroom-lined halls in the building were about two hundred and fifty feet long and featured a twenty-foot wide passage of polished ceramic tile. My office was stuck in an old storage room at the back of the building, right at the end of one of these hallways.

On the day in question, it was ten minutes before the first class, and I heard an incredible roaring noise that seemed to be just outside my office. I couldn't imagine what in hell was happening now. I ran out the door and saw our assistant principle, Lee Sonnaberg, at the far end of the hall wildly waving his arms. He screamed at me "Stop him!"

At that moment a naked eighteen year old boy wearing only a Lone Ranger mask skidded around that distant corner on a big Harley, and accelerated on the tile expanse toward me. The boy and the machine was thundering toward the doors in front of which I was standing.

"Stop him, Hell," I yelled back and ran toward those big doors . I just barely got them open as the masked man roared past me toward freedom. It was a complete coup for that lad. I looked for a silver bullet, but he had left no trace of his identity. In fact, we never discovered who our masked motorcyclist was, but he certainly achieved his purpose of a total disruption of that particular school day.

It was in that same hallway one early morning that I heard girls screaming as I turned that same corner where Lee had stood wildly waving during the motorcycle incident. About twenty feet down the hall was a girl's rest room. A seventeen-year-old girl, apparently unconscious, lay on the floor of the hall in front of the rest room door. As I ran toward the white-faced, inert figure, two other girls flashed out the rest room door and past me, going very quickly in the opposite direction. I pushed into the room and found yet another girl who also appeared to be unconscious just inside the door. "What the hell," I thought. Then I saw it. A twelve-foot long python had wrapped itself around the bars over two of the stalls at the back of the room, and now was fixing his beady eyes and flashing his tongue at me.

Luckily, the girls had just fainted from that frightening sight. The snake's owner didn't claim his pet for about a week. This caused more than a little trouble for our biology teacher who was forced, as a result, to house the great creature in a cage in his small collection of lab animals. A monkey in a cage near the snake fell in love with the reptile and embarrassed more than one of that unfortunate teacher's classes. When the owner finally came to collect his snake, he got not only the reptile, but an unwanted two-week suspension as well.

One of the smelliest student pranks occurred in the spring of 1972. I came in the front door about 6:30 a.m. on a bright morning and was immediately overwhelmed by a god-awful odor. The floor was spotted with piles of manure. As I stood contemplating the scene, a group of large hogs came around a corner at the end of the main hall. Hard behind them came Stoney Mack, our crack custodian.

"What the Sam Hill is this?" I shouted at Stoney.

"Somebody turned sixty hogs in here last night," Stoney answered.

At that moment the building principal, Uncle Tom Mellon, came in the front door. "Jesus H. Christ," he said.

We posted guards outside the doors to keep kids arriving on the first school buses outside. It took forty faculty members an hour to finally herd all the hogs into a grassy courtyard in the middle of the school. Some of our lady teachers seem to resent this early morning duty. It took our janitorial crew an hour and a half to shovel and scrape up the pig manure and scrub all the floors. It took another two hours to find out where the hogs had come from. We discovered that they had evidently been stolen from a farm ten miles east of the school in what must have been a well-planned raid. The culprits had found a door in the high school wood shop open, or, more likely, had shoved a board in the door the night before so that it wouldn't lock, and then unloaded their cargo into the building late at night. It took another week to discover the students responsible for this prank. They proved to be the same all-state football players who had set up the breakfast for my sunrise service. They said that since they were about to graduate, and they wanted to make one last tribute to the place. We never forgot that odorous tribute or the organizers thereof.

Drugs also came to Windy Gap in 1972. As near as we could tell, they came in with that year's sophomore class. The kids in that group seemed to have picked up LSD and marijuana addictions in junior high, and brought them with them to high school. We had more than our share of over-doses, and the sirens and red lights of ambulances became commonplace around our country school.

Our rather idyllic school world was totally shattered when the ambulance crews were too late to save two girls who were found unconscious on the football field. Drugs and alcohol were rapidly replacing obnoxious pranks as the order of the day for our student population. With drugs came the need for money to buy drugs. Open prostitution for drug money also became a feature of life at Windy Gap High. The times, they were a changin'.

About three weeks before we were to leave the old school and move to our new mansion on the hill south of the city, we were hit by a flood. It had rained hard for three days, and then there had been a cloudburst up the canyon, which opened onto the city. As I drove to work on the morning of the great flood, two feet of water rushed and foamed by me on the road, but I thought that it certainly wouldn't reach our school four miles away. I arrived at the building, and there was water everywhere. I forced open the front door of the school and found our principal and the district superintendent standing in calf-high water in the main hall. The brown, cold stuff was running like a river toward all parts of the building. The two administrators looked to be in a state of shock.

"What should we do?" the super asked the principal. Our principal,Tom Mellon, made no reply, but just looked completely puzzled.

"For Christ sake," I said. "Cancel school for today before the buses get here." I was never smart enough to become an administrator during my long education career.

In 1971 we opened the doors on our new award-winning high school. It was huge, carpeted, and totally inefficient. In addition to new facilities, we had a new type of student. There were 2500 of them, and they were primarily city kids. Their very nature was different from the country kids I had taught for the previous fifteen years they were more sophisticated, more cynical, and less wholesome than the country kids had been. There were also differences in their pranks, but

I did recognize some of the comic and tragic elements I had grown to know in years past. They were still into streaking, drugs, and in riding motorcycles through the building.

One of the most unusual incidents happened the first month that we were open. In the center of our new building was the student center. This huge room was hexagonal in shape like everything in the building. It looked to be as large as a jet- liner hanger. It was about a block long, and two hundred feet wide. In the center was a fifty-foot high ceiling supported by massive concrete columns. Long locker-lined ramps ran down both sides of the student center as the building had been constructed on a rather steep hill. The entry to the building was probably a good fifty feet higher than the bottom of the ramps. These amazing ramps were heaven for motorcycle streakers, but this story is about a prank that was far more imaginative.

The faculty lunchroom lay at the bottom of one of the ramps, and I was just coming out the door from that room after quickly devouring my brown-sack lunch, when I heard a great commotion in the middle of the great hall. I found a group of fifty to a hundred girls gathered in a circle looking upward to the highest point in the ceiling. They were all screaming and squealing. There was a small sky light up there at which they were all looking, and which someone had evidently pried open. I watched as a rope was dropped through and fell to the floor below. One end of the rope remained attached to something fifty feet up there on the roof. A figure appeared in the sky light opening and began to rappel down the rope. It was a boy of about eighteen, totally naked except for a small mask across his eyes. The girls shrilled with peals of feminine excitement as he made his way down the rope. When he hit the floor, they rushed forward, but I was there first. I wrapped my coat around his shoulders, (I later wondered what good that would have done) and led him away from the disappointed girls and quickly to the principal's office at the top of the ramp.

I met that boy again ten years after this incident. There he was, in front of me, working now as a teller in my bank! As I stood there making a deposit and remembering that crazy day, he recognized me and smiled weakly. I laughed, and then he said, "I hoped that you would have forgotten that by now." I told him that were things that a person would never forget

Violence also seemed to be a weekly occurrence in a student body this large. Boys fought. Girls fought - they were the most vicious- and most teachers walked away from all these encounters. My early experience as a teacher had been very different from theirs. I thought that it was the teacher's duty to break up fights. This tendency on my part meant that the squawk box in my room frequently barked, "Mr. Hawke, you are wanted in the student center."

I would put a responsible student in charge and head toward that huge cavern in the center of our building to see what was up. The worst incident was a day when I found a young cowboy dying on the floor at the bottom of one of the ramps. There had been a feud between the jocks and the cowboys for a long time. It culminated with a young athlete shoving a foot-long knife into the guts of the cowboy. There was nothing we could do. He was dead before the ambulance arrived.

Another call to the student center had a more happy ending. It was during the time of what our journalists were calling "Operation Desert Storm", and we all had become more than slightly paranoid about Arab people. My classroom box had squawked again, and I was told by an administrator when I arrived at the top of the ramp that a strange and mysterious figure was roaming about the building.

"He looks like he might be a damned Arab terrorist," the assistant principal said to me. We had

had a flock of bomb threats during that year, and that fact also added to our paranoia. The building must be saved from this terrible threat. I ran down the far ramp and had come only a few yards when I saw him. He was a man dressed in a desert cloak and wearing an Arabic headdress. I jumped him and slammed him hard into a concrete wall.

"Please Sir, he said. I am just looking for my wife."

He was, indeed, the new husband of one of our English teachers. He proved to be an Iranian oilman dedicated to his Moslem faith. I have never lived down this embarrassing attempted rescue of our building and western culture. There you have it. Just a few days in the history of American Public education.

24. A TOUGH START

Student teaching is one of the most difficult, stress-ridden tasks known to man. For sixteen weeks a young man or woman is subject to constant supervision and evaluation from a college supervisor, a building principal, and a cooperating classroom teacher, all of for whom they hope to be performing well for to secure a good recommendation. Prospective teachers hear many suggestions and criticisms from all three supervisors as to how they are proceeding, are subjected to constant testing by the students in the classes they are trying to direct, and seldom, if ever, receive anything close to praise for putting their mind, body, and future on the line. They usually come to the this overwhelming task with little or no knowledge on what is really required to control a class of students, or, more importantly, how to teach them something valuable.

During the course of my thirty-some years in the classroom, I had more than twenty student teachers, and have felt great compassion for all of them. Four of these people remain in my mind as symbols of this most difficult of college credit courses, and as examples of the best of their lot. They not only survived, but also prevailed.

The first on this short list was a young woman named Joanne Ostenberger who student taught for me during my fifth year at Fort Darwin High School. Joanne was in her mid-twenties, had two small children, and had become the wife of a prominent veterinary in Darwin before she finished her undergraduate degree. She came to me for her student teaching requirement as I had had her earlier as a high school student. In other words, she was a far more mature person than most young student teachers are when they are first thrown into the fray.

She took to her new profession like a fish to water, and within a few weeks was controlling and teaching two classes of eighteen year olds as well, or perhaps better than many of my colleagues on our staff at Darwin High School. She took instruction very well, and was mature enough to listen without developing the malady of a bruised ego. Ironically, Joanne never taught, at least during the remainder of my tenure in that school. She was, however, elected to the school board two years later, and suddenly my student teacher had become, in a technical way, my boss. I always felt that this was a waste of a potentially great teaching talent.

James Conover served five stretches in Viet Nam as a weapons repairman for the Marine Corps before he finished college and came to me for student teaching. He had planned to come back home after his first hitch, but then a younger brother had been sent over, and then a year later, yet another brother appeared as an infantryman in that Asian country. Jim felt that it was important for him to remain there as long as his brothers were there, so he re-upped for what was eventually a five-year tour of duty.

During all this time in Viet Nam, his young bride waited for him in the United States. In his time with me (he re-upped for a second semester of student teaching with me) this lad proved his endurance over and over again. Jim brought an authority in manner that precluded him from ever having discipline problems. He also had so much enthusiasm for his task that the students responded with great interest and production. He was one of the most level-headed young men I have ever known, and when he finished his student teaching assignment, I highly recommended him to our personnel director so that he might be hired for our district. My recommendation proved to be the kiss of death, and they rejected him. Two years later, however, he had been hired by the largest school district in Colorado, and within two more, had become department head at the biggest high school in the area. A prophet has no honor, etc…

The third young person I remember fondly was the son of my good friend, Deacon Simmons, who was the basketball coach at Windy Gap High. Rick Simmons had been one of my best high school students, so I was very pleased when he asked to student teach with me at the end of his college training. This young fellow was very bright, and dedicated to his college choice of English literature. It was an extremely nice experience to have a scholar as a student teacher. Rick also quickly developed an excellent rapport with the students. I was further pleased by the fact that he, as Jim Conover had done earlier, asked for a second semester of student teaching with me. Once again, I recommended him to our central administration in order that he be hired for Windy Gap. Once again, they ignored my suggestion, and Rick became an assistant professor of English at UCLA where he remains as a successful educator today. It seems to be that to be turned down by Windy

Gap personnel is the first step toward a much better job.

The fourth in my list of successes is a fellow named James Vincent. This Jim had been a Jesuit priest working on the streets of New York City when he decided that the clergy was not for him, and he came to Colorado to become a public school teacher. My semester of working with him as a student teacher was once more, delightful. He didn't have quite the same disciplinary talents that Conover and Simmons had had, but he had a sensitivity and compassion that allowed him to really relate to eighteen-year-olds.

This time my recommendation did work, and Jim remains today an outstanding teacher in Windy Gap's alternative high school. Well, those are the outstanding ones. For many the strain of the student teaching experience was far too much, and they quickly gave up any idea of working in a public school classroom, and pursued careers in other fields. I have often wondered if there wasn't a better way to ease young folks into teaching, but then I remember my own experiences, and know that that semester of hell is, in some ways, a good preparation for the job that public school teachers are asked to perform year in and year out. The career of a teacher demands a special sort of individual, and anyone going into the profession should probably discover that as early as possible.

25. THE OUTLAW RABBIT

In the very depths of grief and despair, there are sometimes incidents, which happen that help us maintain a level of sanity. At such times of strong emotion, we seem to have a heightened sense of awareness. This tale is about one such time.

Summer and I and our children, Spring and Sage, walked slowly up the front sidewalk of the Ft. Darwin Community Hospital on an early summer day in 1975. We noticed a small, white, female rabbit grazing hungrily at the verge of the hospital lawn under some wild currant bushes. She was neatly clipping the tender young grass down to the root line. That day the sky was a cloudless cobalt blue, and the sunshine brightly illuminated the yellow daffodils and purple iris which bloomed at regular intervals in front of the bushes.

In the midst of this celebration of life by man and nature, my little family faced a most difficult task. We had come to the county hospital to visit my mother, Margaret, who lay inside on a bed with starched white sheets dying of liver cancer. She was a beautiful, loving woman who had consistently used her life to help and care for others, but now lay in great pain with those wonderful brown eyes of hers filled with misery and what seemed to be a plea for release from her ordeal. To me it seemed as if God had abandoned her in her time of greatest need.

Hospitals always depress me, and this one with its memories of family tragedy turned my mood especially black. Inside the two large glass doors at the entrance to the building, there was a large reception room in the center of which was a bar desk governed by two sisters who seemed to be at that station at any hour of the day or night for many years. These desk clerks were the Petty sisters, Selma and Matilda, who were a year apart in age, but looked as if they had been born identical twins. Now in their middle forties, they had been in that job since the hospital was built nearly twenty years ago. Both were tall with exquisitely coiffured blond hair, carefully polished nails, and the very latest in stylish clothes. Obviously, most of their attire had been purchased not in Fort Darwin, but at exclusive stores in the city of Denver, ninety miles away. Platte stores had nothing like this in their limited inventories. The ladies had been behind the reception desk so long that they acted as if they were, indeed, the hospital administrators.

Somehow, we got by them and started down the hall to Mother's room. She was awake and waiting for us. She had great difficulty talking, but her eyes communicated her love. She had been fighting her battle against cancer for several years. Mother had undergone surgery, chemo-therapy, and radiation. She had survived the terrors of modern medicine, all to little or no relief from the disease that was consuming her.

I could not yet face the reality of losing my mother: I could not imagine a world without her. I have always had a hell of a lot of trouble when it comes to losing people I love. On this particular day, she had been given massive doses of pain killer, but seemed not to want to surrender to them until after our visit. We had practically the same conversation that we had had many times before as she lay in hospital beds. "Was she feeling any better?" Of course not, but she smiled weakly and nodded. Then we were silent, and just engaged in the quiet communication that I knew all of us understood

My emotions were getting entirely out of control, and I knew that I must get away for a while. "I'll be right back," I said. As I went back toward the reception area of the hospital, I was aware of a great commotion.

Selma Petty was on the telephone talking to someone in a panic -filled voice. I heard her say, "I've called the police."

Not knowing what to expect, I went quickly out the front door and down the steps toward the main walk-way that led up to the hospital. Coming up this walk was Deputy Sheriff Elmo Cracker, and he had his service revolver drawn. It appeared that he was pointing it directly at me. Elmo was a young man that I had had in class not too many years ago. I remembered that it took him six years to get out of high school. This could become a dangerous situation.

"What the hell, Elmo," I exclaimed.

"Stay back, Rock, he said. "I've come to shoot a wild rabbit that has the girls inside in a dither."

Envisioning a bullet through the glass door of the hospital or worse yet, one through me I said, "Put that damn thing down. That rabbit is unarmed."

Elmo looked at me with a state of total confusion, but he holstered his revolver. I glanced toward the base of the currant bushes where Elmo had now fixed his gaze. The white rabbit was still there peacefully munching the tender grass. I reached down and grabbed her by the scruff of the neck, and in doing so, pulled her back from an imminent visit to rabbit heaven.

"I've got her, Elmo. "I'll take care of her."

" Well, O.K.," he said. Then he wheeled with authority and walked back toward his police cruiser. The tension of the moment now somewhat abated, I began to shake with relief and laughter at the absurdity of the situation. I took the rabbit over toward our '50 Chevy coupe and deposited her unceremoniously on the back seat of our old car. Rabbits are rabbits, small town police are small town police, and death is death everywhere.

I went back into mother's room and told them all a little about the situation. Then I said, "I'm sorry, but this is something that we've got to take care of. We'll be back in a few minutes."

Mother just looked at me with that same understanding and trust which she had always projected. As my family and I walked back toward the coupe, I told Summer about our town. There were lagoons and an irrigation dam on the Platte that were both surrounded by millions of cattails, great old cottonwoods, red-winged blackbirds and dozens of other wild things. It seemed to be a perfect spot to release a very frightened rabbit. A few minutes later, the children cheered and Summer squeezed my hand as the white bunny bounded into the cattails.

Hospitals are many times the most unhealthy place for rabbits, and for that matter, people. There are times, however, that we have the power to change the course of events. It had been an unforgettable day. It was the day that the rabbit attacked the hospital. It was also the day that I knew I must let my mother go. I hope that she also found some peaceful springs and a stand of beautiful trees when she was released.

26. TEAR GAS

1971 was a time of great political turmoil everywhere in America, and Windy Gap was no exception. I had been teaching at Windy Gap High School just a couple of years after ten years out on the prairie, and was amazed at the attitude of revolution on the part of the part of both the high school and college student bodies.. These were kids who should have been thinking about the next concert, ball game, dance, or algebra test. Instead they considered themselves part of the anti-Viet Nam movement, as most had fathers, brothers, or uncles who were there, or at the least, television sets which graphically portrayed the body count of enemy dead every night just at dinner time. Televised marches and protests also stirred them. So I guess that I shouldn't have been surprised at the effects showing up in the school populace. Most of the high schoolers were too young for the draft, but got into the anti-government spirit by protesting and demonstrating against everything the high school was trying to do for them. The high school teaching staff and administrators were the government to them. Any authority figure was suspect in their minds. Now, twenty-five years later, the general populace in America seems to have slipped into a similar adolescent fight against law and order.

My family lived just a few blocks from a Junior high school where Sage was enrolled, and our yard backed onto a turnpike between Windy Gap and Denver. We lived in an area where we had to get onto the pike every morning to take Sage to school. In the process of this driving maneuver, we encroached on the edge of the university campus.

On an April morning of that year, Sage and I started out for school. I always dropped him off at junior high on my route to Windy Gap High School. There were hundreds of college kids at the intersection where we had to turn onto the highway, who were trying their damndest to shut down this major artery to Denver. More hundreds filled the walk overpasses between the college and our neighborhood. They were banging on the metal guardrails and shouting anti-war slogans. Sage was then thirteen years old, and had never before witnessed a protest of this magnitude.

He asked me ."Dad, are they really as angry as they seem?"

"Yes", I replied. "But many of them don't really know who they are angry at, or why." Somehow we wove our way through the chanting kids, and I dropped Sage off for another seventh grade day. I ran into groups of marchers with banners converging on the turnpike on my way south to the high school. They seemed obsessed with shouting the "F" word at me as I drove along. I don't know if they were soliciting or simply had limited vocabularies. Obviously there would soon be thousands at the demonstration, and they would, indeed, shut down traffic on the highway.

Later that day I learned that they had blocked the pike and had gone on a rampage of destruction in the small business district near the campus. We also heard that the National Guard had been called out to restore order, and that the highway patrol and local police department were making hundreds of arrests. Helicopters had been brought in to drop canisters of tear gas in an attempt to break up the demonstration.

When I got home that evening, Sage was already there. He had been out on the junior high playing field when the helicopters dropped the gas. Great clouds of that substance had drifted over the little kids playing ball near their junior high. All of the kids in the gym classes evidently were temporarily blinded by the clouds of gas, and many were nauseated. They certainly didn't understand why their army had done this to them. I had a very difficult time trying to explain to my son why this incredible thing had happened. "When excited and self-righteous kids protest something, the crowd can very quickly become a mob," I told him. "In that mob-like atmosphere, both sides do things that are terribly ill-considered, It was just an accident that your school was hit."

"You mean that the government was doing a little to us like they are doing to innocent women and children in Viet Nam," he replied. I quickly realized that he was remembering the chants of the college students who were more important models to his age group than parents or governments. I didn't say any more, but wondered if this experience would someday make Sage another one of those protestors. It didn't. He is now an advocate of law and order, and serves as an attorney for the U.S. Fifth Circuit of Appeals (my personal fears have been allayed) but for some reason our nation has become a veritable hotbed of mindless protest.

The disease of the seventies was highly contagious, and now, in 1996, has apparently spread throughout our population. Twenty-five years ago we had an enemy to focus on. Perhaps now in 1996, the absence of a clearly established enemy has made Americans turn on their government and themselves. Pogo was right.

27. JOHN BIRCH, THE DRAGON, AND MOSES

Men in trench coats sitting in my classroom with tape recorders was not something I ever anticipated as a young teacher. However it happened, and this story tells how and why. During all my college years I had felt that an area of literature overlooked in the public school curriculum was that of the <u>King James Bible.</u> During my graduate studies I took courses in both Old and New testaments, and thereby became certain that this was some of the grandest literatures ever produced by mankind. I read everything that I could find about the history and culture that spawned these great works. I spent a lot of time trying to get as broad of a perspective as I could manage. I remained amazed, and delighted, and reverent after all that study.

Finally, in 1970, I had the chance, as head of the English Department at Windy Gap High School, to put together a new curriculum for our new school. I spent two summers doing more reading and organizing, and in the fall of 1971, I had a new course ready to go. The student response for the course was overwhelming. I had hoped that enough kids might register so that I could teach one section, but more than 100 students said that this new course was their choice, and I thereby had 3 sections of <u>The Old Testament as Literature and History</u> the very first time it was offered. My approach to the material was to humanize it somewhat, and to present it as the real literature and history of a real people, and further, to try to find enjoyment and wisdom in our studying of it. I found as I presented this material to my eager students, that he great book, itself, accomplished all of these goals.

Things went along quite well for about a month, and then I started to have adult visitors coming to class. I always encouraged these kinds of visits as I felt it important that the community know what the public schools were doing. The first to visit were fundamentalist preachers who listened quietly and were non-committal. Next, I had a parade of the major church ministers, priests, and rabbis. They were interested in what we were doing, and, for the most part, supportive. I began to think the community public relations battle was won, and the class might be allowed to continue.

The students seemed to enjoy the class a great deal as we not only studied literature and history, but also did individual in-depth research projects on what each student thought was most interesting about the material, or on subjects they wanted to know more about. Many told me that they had been agnostic when they entered the class, but had found more than enough to make them devotees of the literature and its wisdom by the end of a semester of study.

The second semester saw the classes grow to four, and then from the second year on, we had 200 students each semester ask for the class. I found myself teaching this one subject area nearly full time now. Late in the fall of the second year, two gentlemen appeared at my classroom door one morning, and asked if they might sit in. They were of a rougher sort than the clerics who had visited earlier. They worked at taking notes and running a tape recorder during my lecture and the subsequent discussion. After class they came to my office and said that this kind of thing could not go on any longer. They left me some Ku Klux Klan material and disappeared out my office door without further comment. I was amazed that the Klan was still alive in Colorado.

About two weeks later three fellows in trench coats, each carrying a tape recorder, were waiting for me when I met my first class. They were to make about a dozen subsequent visits, and I really didn't know for a while if they were FBI, CIA, or something else until one day when they stayed after class, and told me that they represented the John Birch Society, and were considering legal action to stop my atheistic activities. I was dumbfounded, as I had worked very hard at being religiously non-committal about all the material we covered. I certainly never put forth any opinion on a religion or a religious belief, and I squelched any student comment that was in any way derogatory to any religious belief.

In the weeks that followed, I had visits from several curriculum experts based at the Windy Gap central administration office who undoubtedly were following up on complaints from my visitors or those that they talked with about their visit. I also began to receive phone calls and written notes from some parents about my teaching the literature of the Devil. A few kids said they couldn't stand it anymore, and dropped out of class. However, during all of this harassment, the great majority of kids remained enthusiastic, and many told me how much they appreciated the class.

Before the third year of this class began, our building principal called me in, and said that he wondered if we should continue to offer a class that engendered so much public criticism. He thought that we should think seriously about dropping the course for the good of the school. I was devastated. Like a rainbow appearing in the clouds, the other side of this controversy suddenly came forward. Happy parents told the principal how valuable they thought the class had been for their sons and daughters, and that fall over 400 kids indicated on their registration slips that they wanted to take the course.

We had been saved. The Birch society and the KKK still occasionally made complaints, but the school board, the central administration, and the building principal left me alone. Moses had defeated the forces of reaction. The upshot of all this sound and fury was that for the next twenty years I taught the class dozens of times to literally thousands of students. It was the most rewarding academic experience of my thirty-three year career in the public schools. After all, this was the world's greatest literature, written by, some say, the world's greatest authors, and all of that was supplemented with the history of the most amazing peoples in the Middle East.

I send this message to all the teachers of the United States. Wherever you are, whatever the circumstances, if you know that what you want to teach is important and needed by your students, don't bow to the pressure of the lunatic fringes. An army of good folks will appear and save you from the dragon.

28. SPRING BREAKS A LEG

Our daughter Spring decided in junior high that her main extra-curricular activity was going to be drama. She was, and is, a very attractive, sensitive young woman, and the goal of becoming an actress seemed to be very appealing. It was a very perceptive choice on her part as her participation with her peers on the stage gave her confidence and poise beyond her years. She had roles in "The Ransom of Red chief," The Wizard of Oz," "The Snow Queen," and "The Dark of the Moon'. She understudied the lead in "The Admirable Crichton," and was a student director for "Camelot."

As recognition of her long and dedicated association with drama, she was elected to the International Thespian Society as a junior in high school. That wasn't, however, her crowning achievement with this activity in high school. As a senior she won the coveted role of Elsie Carmichael, the dipsy ballerina, in "You Can't Take It With You." Finally she had the lead role, and she ran with it. Her performance as Elsie was inspired, and won her applause from her peers, the director, and several audiences during the play's run.

Naturally her parents were very impressed, and we suddenly realized that our little girl had grown up. Driving her to all those practices, picking her up late at night at the end of rehearsals, and suffering with her during times of uncertainty were suddenly worth our effort, and more. For Spring, this success gave her a place in the sun, and peer recognition from a student body of about 2500. It was at a cast party that she met her future husband, Guy Randall. From our grand parents' point of view, without her interest in the stage, there would have been no Jennifer, Mark, and Geoff. Those three grandchildren have become an extremely important part of our lives. I feel certain that the poise, voice control, and confidence she acquired during her many performances has played a big part in her success as a teacher.

For me personally, seeing my little girl strut her stuff behind the foot lights was an experience that I will cherish forever. I not only saw Spring up there, but also realized that she reflected a bit of what Summer must have been like as a performer. An image of the two girls that I love more than anything is overwhelming even at this point in time, more than twenty years later. Spring has used her acquired skills well. Now she teaches literature to high school students, English to adults in the Coconino Community College system, and recently completed a long tour of duty as a member of the Arizona grand jury. More importantly, she has made a home for her husband and her three children. I give her a standing ovation once again.

29. CAPTAIN SAGE

I probably have two of the best kids in the world. They constantly remind me that there are some good genes on my side of the family after all. I know that they have gotten most of their good qualities from their mother, but, in fairness, they must also have inherited the best of the Hawke blood. This little tale revolves around our son, Sage, who started concentrating furiously when he was about four, and then brought that ability to a sport a few years later.

He started playing team football when he was in the sixth grade. Right from the beginning, he was a crackerjack. Sage had shown an ability to develop an all-inclusive intensity that seems to guarantee him success in nearly all the ventures that he becomes a part of. Whatever he lacked in pure physical ability, he more than made up for in determination and intelligence. He had the tools and has applied those attributes all his life.

There is no thrill as complete as seeing one of your children achieve success. My problem was that I wanted total success for him so badly that I was many times too critical of his efforts, and, unfortunately, like many other parents, put far too much pressure on him to reach the goals that I had set for him. Sage, like most sons and daughters, was far more aware of what he desired and what he could do to achieve than I was, or, for that matter, than many other parents are. But enough of this mea culpa, back to what my son really did in football.

Throughout junior high and his sophomore year in high school, Sage was seeking a realistic level of accomplishment; one that would let him achieve excellence, but also one that would not alienate him from his fellows. He found it. In junior high, he had been a hell of a running back. In his first two years of high school football, he became an accomplished nose guard on defense, and a good center on offense. In his senior high school year, his coach made him exclusively an offensive center, a position that I never envisioned for him, but it was here that he found his niche. He also became, in that year, a co-captain of his team. Sage is a fellow who seems to be laid back and quiet, and yet there is an incredible spark there that can make him a tiger at times. His personality turned out to be perfect one for a center. He kept his head in the game, and did his job.

Summer and I always made it a point to attend every one of his games, at home or away. We did it not only to share in his success, but also to make certain that we were there if he was ever hurt. To be honest, we also did it because I didn't trust the judgment of his coach relative to playing his players when they were hurt. I frequently thought that that fellow would do anything to win, and I was going to make sure that he didn't do something that might permanently damage my son. The highlight of his career, in my opinion, came in a game played against our cross-town rival high school one cold November night. Both teams were undefeated, and the winner of this contest would represent our league in the district playoffs. Sage, as offensive center, lined up against a young man on the other team who had been state heavyweight wrestling champion the previous year, and was, reputedly, their toughest player. This fellow hammered Sage with hand slaps to the helmet for the first three-quarters of that game.

On the sidelines Summer and I, and our good friend,Z, sat freezing and disappointed with the beating that our lads were taking. Finally, in the fourth period, Sage, in setting his block at center, locked his hands, and came up with all his strength under the chinstrap of his adversary. He knocked him cold. I was going crazy on the sidelines as they carried the heavyweight champ off the field, and it was only the shouts of my wife that kept me from going onto the field and congratulating him on the spot.

Sage had arrived. I tried to never again tell him what I thought that he should do, but I guess that I must have. Damn, how does one suspend emotion when dealing with progeny? Most times we must understand that kids need encouragement and support, but interference in their lives must be used very sparingly. In the final analysis, all children must perform from their own inner core. It must be the parent's job to give our progeny every chance to develop their own inner strength, and rightly or wrongly, to make their own decisions in life.

30. REVOLUTION

In 1968 a group of faculty members at Windy Gap High School began to meet together and think about what changes they would like to see in our high school educational program. The first things considered were relatively cost-free and included time schedules and curriculum. Then we began to think about a facility that would house these changes. This was the beginnings of our plans for a new Windy Gap High. About a year later the school board and central administration jumped on the wagon. We were then officially underway. We had many ideas of our own, but we also traveled throughout the nation looking at other new schools and systems.

The community then passed a five million-dollar bond issue to fund the building of our new high school. The land on which the new building was to be constructed lay on top of a hill above a lake and a park in the western part of Windy Gap. It was a beautiful site and deserved a beautiful building. Our next responsibility was to plan a curriculum, which would be more relevant to the twenty-first century and would better prepare our graduates for life, and/or college. Many of us had read about a curriculum dubbed the college variable system. This system seemed to offer the flexibility that we desired to implement an expanded curriculum, and it also seemed to promote individual responsibility for the students. The basic idea was to offer a much greater variety of courses, which would better satisfy the needs of a diversified student body. Since we lived in a college town, this curriculum had to prepare youngsters for continuing education at the university level, but it also had to prepare other students who other needs - for community colleges, technical schools, or an immediate entry into the work force. We also wanted to get away from the lockstep of the Carnegie Unit, which had shaped high school curriculums in American for nearly all of the twentieth century. We developed a broad canvas of study which demanded proficiency in the main areas of high school preparation, but would also allow students, with particular interests within those fields, to explore at a much greater depths those things which they were most interested in. We were going from a class offering of about fifty subjects, to a curriculum that offered two hundred and fifty choices.

Naturally such a dramatic change also elicited a good deal of criticism. In addition to all the choices available to each student, the college variable system meant that students would have hours during the week when they might be free of class. A good many parents resisted having us give up our eight o'clock to four o'clock baby-sitting chores. They wanted their sons and daughters accounted for every minute of the school day.

The staff, on the other hand, felt that youngsters in the fifteen to nineteen year old age group, should start to learn individual responsibility. Furthermore we felt that such students should become mature enough to decide when they needed to be at Windy Gap High, or when they needed to be across down at the Vo-Tech school, or when they had free time to work, study in our new complex of libraries and labs, or simply hang out. We also believed that such a schedule would allow teachers office hours within the school day, so that they would be available to individual students for problem solving and enrichment.

Finally, it was decided that we would open with a provisional program, which would be evaluated after three years, and then a decision would be made as to whether or not it would continue. Such a program demanded very different building construction from what we had known in the past. There had to be many more classrooms and offices than were to be found in a traditional high school. We needed to provide an extensive library system, and recreational and enrichment facilities for those students not in class during any particular hour. The implementation of this program also meant an expanded staff which would provide supervision and counseling for our proposed student body of twenty-five hundred kids.

The existing staff really went to work the year before the new building was to open. The ball was in our court, and all of us responded by working fourteen-hour days. I was English department chairman at the time, and, as an example, our staff designed a curriculum of sixty offerings. I was able to work on two classes that I very much wanted to make available to high school age youngsters, -The <u>Old Testament</u> as History and Literature, and Shakespeare: the comedies, the histories, and the tragedies. These types of classes were to be offered in addition to the required composition and general literature classes that students in American high schools had always had available.

Our other main departments, - math, languages, social studies, science, domestic arts, music, business, and physical education also developed

246

highly diversified offerings. Youngsters now could take fourth-year Russian, quantum physics, political science, or bachelor survival, if they so desired. If a P.E. student was interested in lifetime activities, classes in biking, hiking, golf, canoeing, fishing, and tennis were available.

Along with these curricular changes, we also provided a counseling center with ten fully qualified counselors in residence, and satellite department libraries in each subject area for specialized study and research. The main library gave students opportunities not only in basic books, but a great variety of multimedia sources as well. Our plan was rapidly becoming what those veterans on our staff had imagined as the ideal high school.

When we finally got the building open and the classes installed in 1972, many problems developed which we had to handle. The basic design needed some modifications. We found that not all students, and certainly not all parents, could handle such an incredible change from the traditional schools of the past. We had to provide a small part of our students with the old traditional systems of the nineteen-forties and fifties in order for them to function successfully. The open-space classroom design of the building was soon replaced with traditional walls so that teachers and students could concentrate without distraction on their particular classes. Several of the more exotic class offerings were dropped for a great variety of reasons.

However, when the provisional period was over, we received North Central Accreditation and had become one of the best academic-activity high schools in Colorado. We had discovered that it paid great dividends to dream, and then, to implement one's dreams. It was also wise, we discovered, to take a chance and to be just a little different, and sometimes, to fly in the face of convention.

31.THE BRAWL

During my early years at Windy Gap High, my teaching and coaching salaries did not give my family enough money to pay the rent and buy groceries, so I did other kinds of jobs during the time I wasn't assigned to the classroom or a particular athletic team. In retrospect I have often wondered when I did all the other things a husband and father must do - like sleep. One of the "other" jobs that I did was to be in charge of event receipts and crowd control at all Windy Gap athletic events, which did not require my services as a coach. In fulfilling this responsibility, I was usually paid five dollars a night which was, at that point in American history, just enough to take my family out to eat at the university cafeteria.

It was during this period of my life that I felt that I needed to spend more time with my kids, so I took my elementary age son with me whenever I had the ticket business and crowd control duties. This meant that Sage saw an incredible array of high school activity at a very tender age. The coaches of Windy Gap sports took an immediate liking to this youngest, most serious-minded, of the Hawke's, and for several years he became the number one go-for for all of them during game situations.

This particular tale recounts our experience at a basketball game when Sage was about ten. Windy Gap High was in a playoff game with Abraham Lincoln High School, the winner to advance to the state tournament. Emotions were running high for both communities, and the stands were packed with screaming, frantic fans. During the time before the game began, I was very busy selling tickets, marshalling my control folks (teachers and rent-a-cops), and making sure that no blood was shed before the game festivities began. Sage was equally busy serving as ball boy, towel man, and mascot for the Windy Gap Flying Rocks, our very good basketball team. The usual pre-game festivities were in high gear. The cheering squads of bouncy girls in short skirts were inciting their respective groups, the pep band was blasting fight songs off the walls of our gym, and as usual in such situations, no one could really hear anything distinctly. It was the organized chaos featuring sex and violence that exists in gymnasiums all over America from December to April every year. In other words, it promised to be an evening of good old American fun.

Finally the teams were appearing on the floor on the floor to a thunderous reception, the seats were full, and at exactly eight o'clock, the scoreboard buzzer blasted its deafening sound announcing that this most important game was to begin. Windy Gap was coached by an old friend of mine, Deacon Simmons, and his young assistant, Fred "Wild Man" Wilmot. Part of Duke's game responsibility was not only to manage his team, but also somehow keep "Wild Man" under control. Many times I had seen Deacon cram a towel into his assistant's mouth when it became apparent that if the young man uttered one more inappropriate word at the referees, Windy Gap would receive a technical foul.

Lincoln had two young red-haired coaches in green checkered coats who were in their first years of employment. During the game and in its aftermath, I believe they did their best to prevent the trouble, which followed. I have often felt that coaches can control the atmosphere of any high school game, and usually these underpaid, devoted, public servants take that responsibility seriously and keep things well in control. However, this was a most important game for both schools, and the way things developed later, it must have been a night of a full moon. Things were crazy and rapidly getting crazier. Each side had a particularly vociferous fan who added fuel to a fire that certainly did not need a gasoline bath.

There was a loud-mouthed sixty year old grandfather type in the Lincoln contingent who immediately started to demean the Windy Gap players and coaches. On our side of the gym, Rip Simmons, Deacon 's son, who had graduated the previous year, and had been Windy Gap's star basketball performer while he was in high school, was in full throat in support of his father and his old team. Rip answered the Lincoln grandfather's loud comments with retorts of his own. Somehow their respective comments rose above the noise of all the rest of the confusion that night. Aware of what was happening, or could happen, I tried to keep a close eye on my ten-year-old son. He was doing his usual hustling job as go-for for Deacon. I hoped that no matter what happened, the Windy Gap kids and coaches would look out for young Hawke.

For two hours the game thundered along toward its inevitable conclusion. With twenty seconds left, Lincoln led 70 to 69. Windy Gap moved the ball quickly down the floor, our point guard fired the ball to our tall star forward who flung up a desperation shot as the gun went off ending the game. The ball went in. Windy Gap was going to state.

Both stands erupted onto the floor led by Rip Simmons on the Windy Gap side and the screaming grandfather in front of the Lincoln crowd. Rip landed a haymaker on the grandpa who went down like a goose caught by both barrels of a twelve gauge, and immediately there was a full blown melee. As I rushed out in the midst of this mob searching for Sage, I heard a feminine scream and turned to see a young teenager on the Lincoln side get pushed off the top of the stands and fall twenty feet to the floor below. This terrible incident should have brought every one back to their senses, but it seemed tragic that the animal mob on the floor ignored the girl. Later I learned that the girl had suffered two broken legs and a concussion, but I couldn't get through the crowd to help her at that point. I was thrust by a hundred bodies out toward the middle of the gymnasium.

Then I saw Sage. I shoved my way toward him, scooped him up, and turned to try to get to an exit when somebody landed a terrific smack on my ear. Still holding my son, I flattened a fierce face immediately in front of me, and as he fell, I got Sage to a door and out of the mob . I set him down in a safe place with the admonition not to move. I looked back toward the fight and happily saw that a dozen security teachers and the rent-a-cops were in the midst of the fight and seemed to be in the process of shutting down this insanity. I made my way toward the girl who had fallen. She was unconscious and bleeding, and ringed by a group of Lincoln people who didn't seem to be doing anything to help her. However, someone had already called for an ambulance, and within minutes, paramedics had the girl strapped to a stretcher and were taking her out into the night toward an ambulance which had backed up tightly against the front doors of the gym.

The brawl was over almost as quickly as it had begun. Cool heads on both sides had finally prevailed and some were leading the hottest combatants out of the gym, and in many cases, literally throwing them into cars in the parking lot. I stood in the middle of the gym floor shaking with both fear and anger. One of my principals came up and said, "How did you let this happen?"

I just looked back at him in disbelief and anger, but couldn't answer. Sage was by my side now, and we made our way to the lobby where I stared locking doors as soon as areas were evacuated. Later that same night as my son and I made our midnight run to a local bank to put the game's receipts into a night depository slot, He said, "Dad, that was a great game. Coach Simmons gave me two oranges at halftime. Thanks for getting me out of the middle of that fight. You really smacked that guy."

I said, "I'm glad you're okay. What happened there tonight should never happen at a high school game." But I knew that it would happen again in schools all over our country. It is the nature of the beast..

32. FORT FUMBLE

To many in every community, the superintendent of schools is a person representing great erudition and even greater dedication to a most worthwhile cause. Interestingly, the role of this community leader has changed dramatically during my thirty-three years as a teacher in the public schools.

When I first entered the classroom in the 1950's, not only was the super regarded as somewhat of a great leader, but also he or she was perceived as a protector of the classroom teacher whose job it was, in turn, to protect and educate our nation's most precious commodity, our children. The superintendent was not only an educational model for all the lesser lights in professional education to follow, he was also looked upon as an advocate against the critics of the system who always seemed determined to cut educational funding in order to lower their taxes, and, in the process, keep teachers in a financially disadvantageous position so as to make them subservient to the community folks who had a "real" job, and who, "really worked" for a living. The fifties and sixties superintendents not only fought these critics, but also understood the needs of the classroom. They usually worked diligently to supply teachers and students with the necessary materials of education.

In the 1970's superintendents nationwide seemed to discover that there was no way they could do their job without building huge central administration buildings, and then surrounding themselves with scores of assistants who were to exist as an impenetrable wall between the super and the community and its schools. With this large group of consultants, directors, associates, assistants, and their virtual army of secretaries, could a super really be blamed for what happened in the schools? Directors of accounting, budget, business, curriculum, instruction, personnel, employee services, maintenance, payroll, planning and engineering, pupil services, research and evaluation, security, staff development, transportation, warehouse operations, and at least twenty other specifically designated areas, each staffed with a director, an assistant director, consultants, coordinators, and attendant herds of secretary were created. The central administration offices were now housed in almost as many buildings as the school district had schools, and the central staff began to number into the hundreds.

There were now more support personnel and administrators than there were teachers. The superintendent became the chief officer of this crowd of non-classroom personnel, and further distanced himself from teachers and students, which after all, had once been the real reason for a school district. This new organization also changed the face of school boards who became much more political in nature. Each board member changed from being someone in the community who was willing to work many unpaid hours for the betterment of education generally, to being an representative of a particular group or lobby who had a definite agenda that would satisfy their goals. In districts of any size, tens of millions of dollars were at stake, and it seemed as if there were many groups within the community that elected board member to expedite their personal agenda

In the late eighties and nineties, the super's role changed once again. He became an obvious politician divorced from the schools themselves, now representing the school board, community groups, and the businesses of the area rather than the instructional staff and the students enrolled in the schools of the district. This new type of superintendent saw the needs of these lobbying groups to be far more important than teachers and students, and schools. A deputy superintendent was appointed to run the central administration staff. This position undertook the duties, which had traditionally been the superintendent's. More Director positions were created to head up geographical areas (or collections of schools with a district).

The new bureaucracy was now nearly complete. Suddenly there were literally hundreds of people between the classroom operation and the superintendent. Ironically, most of them had never been and were never would be directly connected with, or concerned with the real business of teaching and learning.

I feel that this progress toward the isolation of the teacher and the teacher's classroom of students is directly responsible for many of the problems we perceive in modern public education. A new realization began to surface in the ranks of teachers. We began to know that if there were a way to screw up any aspect of education, the central administrative offices would find it. It was then that we began to refer to the central administration offices as Fort Fumble. Not only does this development of an incredible bureaucracy increase education costs dramatically, it will probably lead to the destruction of the public schools system as we used to know it. It is against this background of organizational insanity that I want to tell you about some of the superintendents I have known through the last five decades. I think that the villains in this situation were first and foremost, greedy and stupid chief educational officers. That is, the superintendents themselves. However, politicians, university schools of education, and unscrupulous and petty parents and parent groups are also to blame. Every time a small group with very personal concerns appeared, a new educational division was created. Perhaps all of this is just a microcosm of our federal government and America on the eve of the twenty-first century.

Oh yes, there are some good superintendents. I don't want to give the impression that all our local educational leaders are incompetent. Some are great people with a real vision, and with compassionate and intelligent views of society.

Unfortunately, I haven't met many of this type. When I came to the Windy Gap school district, we had a succession of the old-fashioned paternal type of school administrators. My first two superintendents there, Alex Frederick and Warren Barnes, were both men who had been in education for at least forty years, and both were just learning about the revolution in school administration which was leading to the development of huge local bureaucracies. Both of these men were basically good people, but had developed the petty tendencies of defense and control which they evidently felt protected their appointment by the school board. Other than those small flaws and their sometime lack of vision, I had no real quarrel with them.

Then Dr. John Farnsworth came to town. He was the first of the new breed of educational leader that has become common throughout America. Part preacher, part politician, John used his folksy personality to charm and delight the school board and nearly all of our powerful community groups. All things considered, I think that Farnsworth did less harm to our district than most of the men who later succeeded him. He was a pragmatic sort of fellow who seemed to actually weigh carefully his decisions as to whether or not they would be beneficial to the children of the district. His one glaring deficiency was his lack of an ability to communicate with classroom teachers and his somewhat shortsighted dedicated to the creation of a super bureaucracy of underlings to protect himself from criticism and rejection. Big central educational offices with hundreds of non-teaching employees were a most desirable thing for him.

The next superintendent in line was George "Man-Tan" Parkins. Superintendents are somewhat like presidents; they rarely stay for more than a term or two. Parkins was a personality boy, and got his nickname because he obviously used a great deal of the artificial skin coloring product. In fact, we speculated the he had a tank at home where he dipped himself at the end of the day in the office. When his skin started to become an unhealthy white in the middle of winter, he would suddenly appear the next day as a deeply bronzed individual, much as if he had suddenly become a Cheyenne Indian brave.

George was a hit as speaker at women's clubs. He was handsome, and had a charming, boyish personality. This charismatic fellow was a public relations expert, but lacked the common sense necessary to run a district. He instituted the perks of huge life insurance policies for the supers paid for by the district, a new car provided each year for the district's main officers, and travel and vacation expenses as a part of the annual administrative contract.

George's main flaw was that he somehow acquired a case of terminal stupidity. He was the man who stood in three of water one flood day in a local high school, and who was unsure as to whether he should call off school that day or not. George moved on to become a superintendent in southern California just two years after winning that position in Windy Gap.

Maybe he is one of the reasons that California has had so many problems in recent years.

The other side of the coin, does indeed, exists. The next superintendent in my ledger of leadership was a man who had come up through the ranks and risen to the position of Deputy Superintendent. He is "the" good example of modern educational leadership. I had worked side by side with Bill Alles as a English teacher, then counselor, assistant principal, and finally principal of the high school where I taught in Windy Gap. Bill is a very intelligent, compassionate man who I have always had great respect for. He is the exception to the rule as far as central administrators are concerned. When a previous superintendent of our district left suddenly, Bill jumped into the job and performed admirably. The district finally began to concentrate on the business of educating children under this man. Fort Fumble appeared to be going out of business. However, his tenure lasted only one year. The school board evidently felt that he was too competent, and replaced him with an accomplished politician.

The school board was smart enough, however, to give him back his old deputy job, where he continues to do the real leadership job for our district today. Bill is the fellow responsible for the day-to-day operation of the district. This allows the new politician-superintendent to play his manipulation games with the school board and community, to control the teaching staff of our district with his carefully prepared press releases in the local newspaper, and to continue to build an almost impenetrable number of assistants and directors who can take the blame for any failure or problem in the district.

Education is like all other areas of society in America. We seem to be terribly short of competent leaders and more than willing to put up with the building of huge bureaucracies.

33. THE YEAR THE ROOF FELL IN

We had suspected the crazy construction of our new high school in Windy Gap for several years. Although the building design had won many national building awards, it seemed obvious to us who worked there, that in many ways, it was a gigantic pile of junk. Thirty inches of wet snow proved that our worries were justified one Saturday morning in January of a very cold and wet winter. There were a large group of students taking a college entrance exam in our cafeteria, when our head janitor came to our principal, Bill Vannoy, and told him that there was something going on the roof that they better look into.

The two men climbed fifty feet up ladders to the roof of our building and walked across to the suspicious area. Just as they were about to step down on it, 3000 square feet of ceiling and a dozen massive pre-formed concrete supports crashed down to the floor of the student center.

Luckily, the cave-in missed the two hundred kids taking the ACT exam by just a few feet, but the collapse of the roof was to close our building for months. The structural damage done was to take nearly two million dollars to repair. Law suits against the construction firm and the architect were in the courts for years, but finally, a settlement was reached that paid for the reconstruction. Initially, school was completely out for a week as the faculty met to go into the rubble and retrieve important documents in the classroom section of the buildings. Many of the concrete pillars remaining in that section had been badly cracked in the cave-in, so this was careful and tedious work. We also had to decide how to continue our Spring semester schedule in a different location.

For several days the faculty and administration met daily in church basements around our community to decide how we were going to handle this disaster. Not only classes, but also basketball games and wrestling matches, a play, and several concerts had to be rescheduled for new locations. The University of Colorado offered us classroom space, and the other high school in town said that they would somehow squeeze us into their gymnasium and auditorium schedules. We were to become a high school temporarily without a home, and found ourselves scattered around Windy Gap in whatever locations the community could find for us.

There were a great many positive and negative results from this situation. Since we were now totally decentralized, a great many attendance problems raised their ugly heads. Kids said that they missed class because they couldn't get transportation, or couldn't meet the strange time schedules we had to institute in an effort to use space when it was available. In most cases, I felt that the distractions of the university campus were just too much for some high schoolers to

handle However, there were some positive elements :
our seniors got an early look at what lay ahead of them
on the college campus, and were thus better prepared
when their turn for advanced education came the
following year. Another positive was that for the first
time since I had been at Windy Gap, the high school
faculty got to know and work with the college faculty.
This opportunity was certain to pay dividends in future
years.

Perhaps most positive of all, all of us - teachers,
students and administrators - discovered that we were
capable of far greater flexibility, and we also discovered
that in the face of a disaster, we could pull together,
and not only survive, but prevail. It turned out to be
a real confidence builder for us all. Most satisfying of
all the results from this occurrence was the fact that
fat cat architects and construction contractors not only
had egg on their face, they had a whole omelet. I have
often wondered what they did with those trophies they
had received for building design and construction.

At that point in time, I was burned out as a teacher and as a man. My health had begun to fail, and like our building, my own roof had fallen in. I felt old and tired and sick. I knew that my turn to leave the profession had to come soon.

Claude M. Higgins, Jr.

PART FOUR
MEMORIES OF FAMILY AND FRIENDS

Claude M. Higgins, Jr.

34. TO DURANGO AND BACK THE HARD WAY

One of my family's very first family vacations involved a trek diagonally across most of the Colorado mountains. Our goal was to visit the ruins at Mesa Verde in southwestern Colorado. In addition to our children Spring and Sage, Summer and I decided to bring our two Siamese cats along on this trip. Mother Mitzi's kitten Violet (known to us as Pookie because she was such a crazy little cat) was just three months old, and an adorable little cream colored animal with dark points and bright blue eyes. We stopped many times on the trip to walk the cats on strings tied to their collars. Invariably we heard, "Oh, it's a mama and a baby."

Spring was eleven and Sage was an active eight years old at the time of this trip. We drove south from Denver to Bailey, and over Kenosha Pass to Fairplay and Buena vista. This route is a remarkably beautiful drive that includes high mountains, pine forests, and lush meadows. From Buena Vista we climbed over Monarch Pass, and then slipped down through the Black Canyon of the Gunnison River. We stopped in the college town of Gunnison for a roadside lunch of bread and lunch meat. We had already been on the road for eight hours. Summer and the children sang songs, Spring delighted us with her constant puns, and the cat girls alternately slept and romped around the car. I just held my eyes on the road, and hoped that perhaps we were making some headway toward our goal. By three in the afternoon we were by the great blue lake called Blue Mesa Reservoir, and stopped in the western slope town of Montrose for a little ice cream and a few minutes of rest.

The Siamese appreciated the soft ice cream as much as the humans did. The August day had now heated up to about eighty-five degrees. We turned south at Montrose, and soon had driven through many more mountains and the picturesque towns of Ouray, Telluride, and Silverton. As we started up Red Mountain Pass toward Durango, we noticed that clouds were gathering on the high mountains. Five miles from the summit we hit a thunderstorm that soon turned to a blizzard of hail. The hail piled up on the road, and I struggled to keep our old car from sliding off the edge of the highway, and down a thousand feet into a yawning canyon. Finally the storm abated into rain again, and we saw the first roadside sign advertising that it was eighteen miles to Durango. It seemed as if we drove five miles farther, and then we saw a sign, which read seventeen miles to Durango. This ridiculous pace continued on and on. After about forty minutes, we noticed a sign that said four miles to Durango. Great! We were just about there. Twenty minutes later the roadside sign read one mile to Durango. Summer and Spring, and Sage were totally exhausted. The cats had become increasingly peevish, and I was almost at the point of not really giving a damn one way or the other.

But then, as advertised, here was the town of Durango. We found a motel, unpacked, ate more bread and dog meat, and were just planning to get a relaxing shower when the power went off. We were in a strange town, in a strange motel, and we were so tired we really didn't know which end was up, and now the damn lights were off for two hours, and we found ourselves in the kind of total darkness that one finds only in the mountains. We had been on the road that day for sixteen hours. What a way to end the first day of our vacation!

In the morning, after a good restaurant breakfast, we started off for Cortez and the cliff dwelling ruins at Mesa Verde. We spent a delightful morning climbing around the ruins of what apparently was a highly sophisticated Anazasi civilization of a thousand years ago. Spring got very nervous on the ladders, but with Summer ahead of her, and me behind, we pulled and shoved her up and down several thirty-foot high primitive ladders.

By ten thirty that morning we started back to the east. The first obstacle was Wolf Creek Pass, one of the most difficult drives in all of America. However, we negotiated the pass without incident, and began our drive through the San Luis Valley. The towns of Pagosa Springs, Monte Vista, and Del Norte came and went. We stopped near Alamosa for a late lunch, and then turned north toward Salida. The stretch between Alamosa and Salida is one hundred and ten miles of absolutely nothing but sagebrush along a road that runs as straight as any string. We drove it very fast under a threatening sky, and felt when we reached Salida as if we had had just come through the Twilight Zone. We found a good motel in Salida and had a wonderful, hot meal in a restaurant.

The next morning, day three of our trip, we drove east to Canon City and visited the Royal Gorge. Outside of this area we came to the Hayden Creek Campground and had one of the most restful lunch breaks of our trip. We walked the cats on their strings, and had more bread and lunchmeat. Sage and I walked out on the bridge over the Royal Gorge and looked down at the river and rocks a thousand feet below, but Summer, Spring, and the cats decided to pass on that opportunity.

From the Gorge we drove east through Florence and Pueblo, and then turned north toward our destination for that day, Colorado Springs. We found a motel in yet another thunderstorm complete with downed power lines on the road, showered, and had a sit- down supper, and went to see the movie "Cat Ballou." Day four dawned clear and beautiful. We drove up to Cheyenne Mountain, and had a great time visiting one of the most interesting zoos in America. We started back for Fort Darwin in mid-afternoon and arrived while there was still a little daylight left. We had covered about sixteen hundred miles of up and down driving, made stops to see a dozen attractions, put up with incredible storms, kept two cats safe on their strings, and all of this in four days on about $400. Such was life for a teacher's family in the mid-sixties. But we had a heck of a vacation.

35. CAT TALES

Our daughter Spring was a sweet, innocent, beautiful child who secretly kept small needle-sharp claws sheathed inside velvet paws (her method of attack was, as it is today, the quietly delivered "zinger" which left her victim temporarily unaware that they had just been zapped). Spring had tight dark curls, beautiful big brown eyes, and a lady-like posture as a two-year old. Although now a mature mother of three, her physical appearance hasn't changed that much. It was only natural that her pets of choice would be cats. Cats are quiet, mysterious, extremely agile beasts. Their general demeanor seemed to exactly fit our little Spring. At the age of two she acquired her first cat - a black rascal tom named Imper. Imper had watched too many Roy Rogers' movies which led to his favorite pastime of leaping from terraces onto the back of other unsuspecting toms, and then wresting them down a hillside, the two cats rolling over and over in a cloud of fur until they reached a precipice over which they would drop into a heap.

My memories of this first of Spring's cats centers around a urinary disease which the tom had undoubtedly acquired from his many fights. We were very poor at the time, and I remember my wife, Summer (who didn't like highway driving) driving this cat fifty miles to the state veterinary college at Fort Collins so as to receive free treatment for the young fellow. Imper eventually succumbed to his many wounds, and joined that big cat fight in the sky, but he remains as the first in a long line of interesting animals who shared our daughter's bed.

Her second cat was a black and white shorthair farm cat given to her on her third birthday by her Uncle Bill. Bill doted on his little niece, and delivered with obvious joy this kitten with a big green bow tied around his neck to Spring on her fifth birthday. She named him Frosty. Frost was an extremely loyal and loving cat to his mistress, but he terrorized the rest of the cat population of Fort Darwin. He somehow could effect a facial expression that had to remind people and cats, if they were film watchers, of Lee Marvin at his nastiest. His fighting expression could be described as a threatening, insane leer. He would be absent from our house for three or four weeks each year during which time he fathered many, many more black and white kittens all over town. He had an unusual way of fighting. He would cock his head to one side and advance slowly toward an adversary fixing them with great tiger-eyes. A re-telling of some of his battles is appropriate.

Once a large white tom made the mistake of coming up on the porch of our house. Frost grabbed him and stripped away a two-inch swath of fur all the way around the poor beast's neck. With a great pink strip of flesh exposed, the intruder barely escaped Frost and more terrible damage.

One other night I heard the sounds of cat war, and raced outside to see Frost run a large Siamese tom full speed into the side of a nearby house, knocking the cat into an unconscious state. In the helpless condition of his current enemy, Frost then leaped on him and tromped him into total submission.

Perhaps his funniest encounter (in a messy way) was one morning when a young gray tabby tom came through an open back door into our house. Frost met him in the living room, cocked his head and advanced. The apparition approaching frightened the intruder into a state that could be described as "scaring the shit out of him." Cat stuff flew everywhere around the house until we could open the front door and let that terrified beast escape.

Frost had other abilities as well. There were many mourning doves in Fort Darwin. Frost came up with a strategy to capture these lovely Grey birds. He would crouch over an anthill pretending to study the movement of the insects. Curious doves would gather on the telephone wires to watch this amazing activity. Soon one of the bird's curiosity would get the better of him, and he would swoop down for a closer look. Frost would wait until the dove was three feet from the anthill, then leap straight up into the air and capture the poor thing with his lightening paws. This strategy made for many dinners of warm dove for the old tom.

Frost, on the other hands, was very mellow with Spring, letting her dress him in doll clothes and be wheeled about in a doll buggy. The face of this warrior cat peeping out from under a frilly bonnet was enough to break up most onlookers. Every night that he was home, he would sleep sweetly beside her in her bed. This scene was another one of those pictures that I have never forgotten.

Next Spring acquired a female Siamese named Mitzi who proceeded to have a litter of five kittens in my underwear drawer. Mitz had a great deal of spirit and determination. She kept her kittens herded within the confines of our back patio with the unwanted help of Sage's dog, Lad. One day Lad snapped at one of the kittens who had approached the dog's dish with the thought of sampling dog food. Mitz, in a maternal fury, drove the eighty-pound shepherd-coyote under and behind a toilet tank where she kept him for hours. Mitz never forgot this affront.

When it came time to give away Mitz's kittens, Spring decided that she could not part with one, a cute little female she officially named Violet, and nick-named Pookie. Mitz and Pook lived for twenty years in our house doing daily ballet performances. The Siamese mother and daughter became inseparable, and could frequently be found sleeping nestled together in a brown and black cinnamon roll shape on a bright orange pillow on our front room couch. Old Mother Mitz knew Lad a Dog, our son Sage's loyal Shepherd-Coyote, was very ill on the night of his subsequent death. For the only time in their relationship, she came up to the sick dog's head and commiserated with him with all her animal compassion as the old fellow lay struggling to breathe on our living room floor.

When Spring was eight she acquired a Maine Coon Cat, a male named Sox for his four white feet. Sox was a very loving and loyal cat who was always by Spring's side. With his great striped gray and white racoon tail held proudly at full mast, Sox was a most distinguished tom cat. I remember well the night that we went out to pick him up at a farm west of Fort Darwin. Spring held the kitten inside her coat all the way home. As soon as she put him down on the floor of our house, the miniature tiger ran across the floor and leaped on our two full-grown Siamese females who had become earlier inhabitants of the Hawke household.

This large cat liked to curl up inside the legs of our sleeping Lad a Dog at night. He also devised a strategy of leading other toms whom he had been fighting around our house, under a gate, and into the jaws of his waiting buddy, the Shepherd-Coyote. Unfortunately, Sox was lost on one of our many moves. We had moved from one side of Windy Gap to the other, and Sox, confused by his new surroundings, attempted to return to his old home. The entire family looked for him for weeks, but we never saw him again.

Spring's next cat was a Siamese tom she named Banzai. Spring had by then become a sophisticated young lady, but she still loved those furry feline creatures. Banz came into our home as a very small kitten and immediately took over the care and protection of the Siamese girls. He rescued them when they got high into trees, showing them, time and again, how to back down when one is trapped thirty feet up. He evidently felt that just giving up and falling twenty feet to the ground was really a mentally stupid action. He also rescued Mitz, who one dark and stormy night, found herself on the other side of a flooded creek that happened to be rolling behind our house and had torn out the foot bridge from the other side. This big Siamese tom heard her distressed meowing, leaped the creek, and then herded her down a block to a safe bridge crossing and back home. All his endeavors at the creek side weren't always so gallant. The Siamese girls, prim and proper with the cleanest of velvet paws, would sometimes sit on the bridge over our creek fascinated with the quick flowing water below. Banz would hide in the weeds near the bridge, waiting until the girls had their full attention on the creek, then he would leap out knocking both fastidious Siamese into the water where they would hiss and meow in full panic. I believe that I often saw him laugh heartily about this joke.

Banz was also a watch- cat driving other cat intruders away from our yard. He loved to ride in the car, but would growl and jump menacingly at any stranger approaching "his" vehicle. Banz succumbed to cancer about a year after Spring had gone away to college. The old Siamese females he guarded so well lived on for many years. Both died in their early twenties long after Spring had begun her career as a teacher. I will never forget the joy and love our daughter exhibited toward her long string of feline pets. She remains today a lover of animals, particularly cats. She has passed this fascination with cats on to her three children. There will probably always be several cats living in her house, and there will undoubtedly be many more in the homes of her children.

There are just a few more cat stories that I want to add to this chronicle. This last section could be titled "Darwin Red, Elm Street Black, and the Girls". We have always been cat people. Oh yes, we have had some very good dogs, but cats have always fascinated both Summer and me. There is something about those mysterious, independent, sleek animals that we find irresistible.

The greatest cat that ever lived with us was a big red tabby tom named Tigger. Tig was Summer's classroom cat. She found him as a half-grown kitten in the furnace room of Darwin elementary. When she first picked him up, he put his front paws around her neck, and she was smitten. He delighted and amazed her fourth -grade class for an entire school year in 1977. His feats became legendary with that class of youngsters.

Because of student allergies in her next class, Tig joined us at home where he was to live with us for sixteen more years. He immediately laid claim to our neighborhood, and paraded daily up and down its sidewalks, his tail held on high as he dared any other tom-cat to challenge his position as top feline. He fought all comers, and we received many panic-stricken calls from other cat owners about what he was doing to their warriors. As far as I know, he retired undefeated after a life-time of ruling our section of town. He was a crusty old fellow, and for some reason or other, hated the people who lived across the street. Every morning he went to their house and sprayed their front door. I don't think that they ever discovered who was giving them this daily insult.

But it wasn't his fighting abilities that made him so special. He was also the world's greatest lover, and he was in love with Summer. He made it a point to sit on her lap every night where he demonstrated his amorous techniques. He would wrap those front legs around her neck, purr in her ear, and give her many cat kisses on the chin. At bedtime he sought the warmth of my beard, and would snore there contently until morning.

He was a great hunter as well. He single-handedly wiped out a large ground squirrel population which had inhabited the meadow behind our house. He decimated both the water snake and frog population as well. There was a big bull squirrel who climbed onto our barn roof daily, and thumped and barked until we would let Big Tig out. These two would run and fight from dawn to nightfall. It was about an even match. I remember finding them one day, locked in a wrestling embrace with their front legs clasped around each other's neck. Their jaws were working in an attempt to sink their teeth into the adversary's neck, but evidently the match ended in a draw.

One day Tig caught the four foot bull snake who lived in our garden. The battle made its way toward an irrigation ditch which borders our property. The snake wrapped its coils around the cat and drug him into the water, evidently trying to drown him. Tig worked free, and ran for his life. He jumped our six-foot backyard fence, and fell into the jaws of the neighbor's Great Dane. That red cat came back over the fence even faster than he had leaped it in the first place. He ran for the house and hid under our bed for two days. When he came out, we discovered a deep snake bite on his chest. A lot of antibiotics and a good vet saved his life. Tigger became very ill in his seventeenth year. We and his vet tried everything, but the old fellow was full of cancer. He was a fighter, however, and hung on for months.

Then the day arrived when he couldn't eat, drink, or even move without pain. We took him in for one final visit to the vet, and he died peacefully in Summer's arms, rubbing his chin on her chin as he went out.

A couple of years after Tig joined us, a terrible apparition appeared at our back door. We didn't know what kind of beast this was. He looked like a discolored wolverine. I tried to drive him off by spraying him with the hose, but he refused to leave. After a few days, Summer began to leave food out for him. This procedure continued for more than a month, and then one day he shot into the house through an open door. He is still here twelve years later. His name is Oneida Black or Shadow, and he is the biggest, sturdiest, black Persian in the county. His discoloration had come from malnutrition. He was starving when he showed up on our door-step. Now that Tig is gone, Shad has become the lord of the manor. He loves one of our new kittens, and wrestles very carefully with her. He is a very good, if very quiet and private cat. Shad's personality is blooming in his old age now that he is no longer subservient to the Tigger. He really is a loving animal who especially enjoys the company of my ancient aunt on her weekly visits to us from the rest home where she lives.

Shadow takes up daily residence in my office, and seems to be quite interested in the business of writing on a computer. He has that short Persian nose and constantly sneezes. Shadow also likes to spend nights out, using his natural color to roam and observe unseen in the darkness. Recently two new red tabby female kittens have joined our household. We call them the Tabitha Spice Girls, and Summer named them Ginger and Cinnamon. We found Ginger at the local humane society in October of 1994. The vet said she was a feral cat, and certainly had never been in a house before. After weeks of hiding, Ginger bonded to Summer, and now is constantly by her side or on her lap. She is a very small tabby cat, with delicate face and paws, and probably will always be about the size she is now at six months. She has never learned to meow, but instead, squeaks. Ginger is a real conversationalist and squeaks to announce her presence, or when she is involved in any activity. Her most amazing trick is to rear back on her hind legs and run through the house like an arctic hare. She is one of the most affectionate animals we have ever had. Cinnamon came to us from Arvada. She had appeared on Summer's sister Marilyn's door step and refused to go away. John, Marilyn's husband, said no more cats, so Marilyn advertised the lost kitty for weeks. No one came for her so, Summer and I decided that we had room for one more.

Cinn is a classic red tabby with a beautiful face. She is very curious, but a joy to have around. She hates closed doors, and throws them open with great aplomb. She and Ginger have become the best of buddies and put on after-breakfast floorshows for us. Cinnamon collects paper clips and rubber bands from throughout the house, and then stashes them under my desk. At night she digs them out and has marvelous games. She also has finally bonded with us and comes to our call like a dog when she is outside. Cinnamon has a great deal of poise, and appears to be a young cat who will soon take over management of our neighborhood. She has already learned to organize the neighborhood squirrels. Well, that's a little about the Hawke cat mania. We wouldn't have had it any other way.

36. THE ADVENTURES OF LAD-A-DOG

It is a strange and wondrous phenomenon. An animal can many times bring a family together and into focus. Such an animal was a part coyote, part shepherd-collie dog which had been dumped in front of Darwin High School. He spent a week in the principal's office, and then Seldom Wright, the school principal, had convinced me to take him home to my family. It was near the time of my son's fifth birthday, and so Lad, as we eventually called him, became a birthday present.

My son Sage was delighted. We misread the dog's sex initially, and Sage called our newest family member Lassie, until Grandpa came over and said, "Sage, your animal is a male." The boy hit his Grandpa in the stomach, he was so disappointed that he didn't have the T.V. heroine. So the dog became Lad-a-

Buck, the Wonder Dog. He was a cute, gold and white furry pup, and grew to be a strong, intelligent, very fast eighty pound dog with a blond back and head, white legs, tail and muzzle. The boy and the dog became inseparable. I will always have the two pictures clearly in my mind: one of Sage and his coyote on the floor of the living room, the dog contentedly asleep as Sage lay beside him rubbing his chest, and then the other mind photo was a family grouping of my wife, Summer, in all her beauty in a sun dress, flanked as she lay on a chaise lounge on our patio, by Spring, Sage, and the noble Lad-a Buck. I think that we were as happy then as a family can be.

From the age of five, then, until Sage went to Colorado College as a freshman, Lad was his constant companion, his resident shrink (sympathetic listener), and his confidant and loyal friend. At that time our family had a Siamese mother cat, old Mitz, who had a wonderful litter of five beautiful Siamese kittens. Lad, little more than a pup himself, decided it was his responsibility to herd and guard these small felines. The mother cat appreciated his help until the day that he snapped at one of the young tom-kittens who had decided that dog food looked like a suitable meal. The enraged Mitzie drove the brave Lad-a Dog behind the tank on the toilet and wouldn't let him out for hours.

One would think that this experience would cool his ardor for herding, but Lad became the greatest herder of cows, horses, and seagulls that Platte County had ever known. His herding of seagulls was particularly interesting. About twenty miles West of Fort Darwin lay Jackson Reservoir. Locales for recreation are somewhat scarce on the prairie, so our family spent many days at this lake, picnicking, swimming, playing on the beach and just hanging out. Lad always went along on these excursions. Lad's first order of business upon reaching the lake, was to set out on a dead run (actually a coyote lope) in an attempt to circle the ten-mile perimeter of the reservoir. Two hours later we would see a speck on the horizon coming from the opposite direction. It was Lad who never broke stride until he had rejoined us on the beach. This obligation completed, he usually spent the rest of the day trying to herd the hundreds of sea-gulls sailing on the blue waters of the lake. Naturally the gulls resisted his efforts, but he persisted in great sun-fishing leaps, trying his darndest to bring all those birds together.

It was also at Jackson Lake that Lad had his narrowest escape. On a cold, bright December day, our family of four and my parents were out getting some mid-winter exercise. Lad, as always, was whipping around us. The lake was frozen, so the dog ran and slid out toward the middle of the reservoir about two hundred yards out from the beach. With a terrible crack, the ice gave way, and Sage's beautiful animal was in the icy water. We all shouted and screamed at the dog knowing in our hearts that he probably was lost. Lad, however, had other plans. After what seemed an eternity of struggling in the freezing water, Lad gathered his strength for one final lunge at the edge of the ice. His strong toes and claws dug in, and ever so slowly, he pulled himself away from a cold, watery grave. There was much rejoicing on the shore.

The golden coyote had two shows that he performed every year of his life. One was his yearly bath. Sage would get out our old washtub, fill it with warm water, gather his big dog up and dump him in the tub. He would then proceed to lather the shivering, miserable animal from tail to snout. Lad's expression was always one of bitter resignation - a hang-dog look, you might say. He then would be toweled dry and came out a golden, fluffy show dog. Naturally Sage was always more wet and disheveled than his animal at the end of this annual ritual.

The other yearly Lad show came every Christmas. We always bought him a present, wrapped it, and put it under the Christmas tree. Lad-a Dog would spend days locating his present, and then guard it until Christmas Eve. On that glorious evening, as all the family excitedly awaited the package unwrapping, the dog would be by his young master. When Sage picked up Lad's present, the dog's enthusiasm could not be restrained. He always began to climb up Sage's frame after his present. It was a struggle to get the box unwrapped and give it to him. Once the gift was secured, he would take it to a corner and hover by it for days.

In the early 1960's our family moved into our first real home - a modern, red-brick, sub-division house that we had bought from my grandfather. In the basement were two bedrooms with a bath in between - the first in-house independence for Spring and Sage. All of this was a great, new luxury for our family, but the basement shower had a problem. Whoever had put in the shower had finished it with sheet rock walls. Knowing that the walls would disintegrate as the shower was used, and not having enough money to tile the walls, I decided on painting them with green epoxy paint. It worked fine. I even had a little paint left over, so I decided to paint the clothes line poles in the back yard. They too looked great. Lad had watched this last procedure and went immediately to inspect them when I finished. His huge, white tail got too close, and he immediately was stuck in the epoxy. In a panic he circled the pole, his tail sticking more tightly all the way round. The only way to get him loose was to cut him free. This procedure left a two-inch ring of beautiful white fur around the pole. Although we have moved far away from this first house, I am sure that thirty years later, that clothes line pole still boasts a ring of fine white fur.

Another family activity was to play baseball. The four of us, followed by two Siamese cats and Lad-a-Dog, would troop to a near-by field. The cats would take up their position behind the back-stop to serve as rooters. The dog would deploy himself in the outfield - he always played all three fields. The games would then begin. We had great family fun until some one socked the ball into the outfield. Like a canine Willie

Mays, Lad would field everything that came his way. The only problem was that he would never give the ball back. Now came his idea of a greater sport - keep away. For the next thirty minutes, or until we ran out of gas, all four of us would run and dive at the dog in an attempt to get the ball. Lad was a grand master in keep away. He would dodge and cut and never be trapped. The game was invariably called because of dog.

Every year in Fort Darwin Lad had to be driven five miles south of town for his annual shots at the Vets. He could be a ferocious dog on occasion, and the veterinarians were scared to death of him. Summer assumed the task of the yearly vet visit, and it was she who worked out a method of Lad getting his shots in such a way as to protect the vet. Lad was to be kept in the car, and the vet would lean in the open window and put the needle in him as Summer held his jaws. This worked fine until one year, when during the mad scramble that always ensued during this procedure, the vet almost gave Summer a shot for canine distemper.

Platte County would be hit by terrible thunderstorms during the summer months in Fort Darwin. The wind would blow, the rain came in horizontally, and the thunder would boom across the prairie. On one such night, Lad was trapped outside the house in the middle of such a storm. A mighty blast of wind overturned the barbecue grill with a great crash, and the steel grill cover came hurtling off and blew directly toward the frightened dog. This traumatic experience produced a predictable future behavior in Lad. Whenever a thunder storm blew in, Lad would run for the safety of our bed where he spent many nights panting nervously beside Summer.

Lad was great buddy to a series of family tom-cats. He always adopted them, and a frequent evening scene was to find a big tom-cat asleep between his paws as the dog slept on the floor. He and Bonzai, our big Siamese tom, also devised a devilish plan for scaring the fur off stranger tom cats. Bonz would get another tom to chase him, and then lead the designated beast around the house toward a back gate set about eight inches from the ground. Lad would be waiting on the other side of the gate, and as Bonz dove under the gate and into safety between Lad's legs, the pursuing tom would run right into the jaws of the biggest blond alligator he had ever seen.

Every night before we brought him in for bedtime, Lad had to patrol his backyard borders. He had worn a path in the lawn just inside the fence all the way around the yard. He refused to come in the house until he had carried out his responsibility of checking every corner of the property. The obligation that he felt for taking care of the family extended to two men who were regular members of my poker club. One was a large, loud, rather obnoxious fellow who Lad, for some reason - probably a legitimate one- always detested. When this fellow came to the front door, we had to lock Lad up, or he would happily have eaten him. He had the same feelings toward a man I had known all my life. Carl was a good fellow who had worked at a local gas station since W W II. He was friendly and polite, but he smelled of oil. This odor sent Lad into a frenzy. Once again it had to be dog lock-up time.

In 1967 our family moved to Windy Gap. My career at Fort Darwin High had hit an impasse, Summer needed badly to finish her teaching degree so that she could do what she was born to do, and we desperately needed two teaching salaries coming in if we were to have any hope of sending our two children to college. Windy Gap had the State University where Summer had completed her first two years of college eleven years before, so the Gap it was. There were many complications in the move. One was that we had no family home for three months, so I took a job teaching summer school in Windy Gap while the family stayed with my parents ninety miles away in Fort Darwin. Lad was housed in a Fort Darwin vet hospital during this time.

Finally, in August of that year, we began our move to our new hometown. On the last trip with our possessions to Windy Gap, we stopped at the hospital and picked up Lad-a Dog. The family station wagon was jammed with boxes leaving only a small space near the tail-gate for Lad. We decided to have the vet sedate the dog so that he would travel quietly in the small space behind all the boxes which, incidentally, were stacked up near the roof for the full length of the wagon. Lad went out like a light, but it had been three months since he had been with his little master who was now ten and growing toward becoming a tall, strong man. After half an hour of traveling, Lad began to revive. As he regained consciousness, he had one thought in mind. Get to Sage. He began a slow, tortuous crawl over the six feet of boxes which separated him from the boy. Finally, after a twenty minute of struggle, he reached the front seat and the wonderful security of Sage's arms.

On the subject of responsibility there is yet one more Lad story. We bought a lot and decided to build a house in Windy Gap, which would become our new family home. All this happened about a quarter of a century ago, but I remember it as if it happened yesterday. The construction of our house took six months. Every night the whole family would go to the site and inspect the progress. Lad, however, was the real building inspector. He would carefully examine every change that was made - from early excavation to the much later closets. He inherently had a sense of ownership and responsibly, and felt the need to check everything belonging to the family. On one visit to inspect the progress on the new house, Lad's herding instincts took over, and he decided to herd a group of mares grazing contently in a nearby field. Everything was going well and the mares were bunching, when across the meadow came an irate stallion who had set his sights on Lad's tail. With teeth bared, the stallion missed robbing the dog of his glorious plume by just an inch or so as Lad made his escape under a barbed wire fence.

When we finally moved into the new house, Lad set to work establishing his new domain. Our property was bordered by a meadow of waist -high buffalo grass which Lad immediately established as his day-time home. We could always find him there by looking for a depression of about ten feet in circumference, which proved to be his nest for the day. On a typical day he would eat breakfast on our deck, and then he began hunting muskrats in Bear creek which ran directly behind our new home. He kept up the hunt until it got hot, and then made his daily nest in the meadow. He usually slept until evening, and then was up again after muskrats. Where he found one, he would dig into the clay banks of the creek trying futilely to catch the varmint. About eight o'clock each night he always came home for supper. Before feeding him, Summer would clean the Grey mask of mud from his face which had daily been plastered there by his tunneling in the creek banks.

This idyllic life lasted four years for the mighty hunter. Lad developed a strategy for guarding his new home from other marauding dogs. A woman who lived across an expanse of meadow and park about four blocks to the west of our new house, had two huge black Labradors which she walked daily in the general direction of our house. They usually ranged about two hundred yards in front of her as the three made their way toward the East. Lad would be waiting. We had built a small bridge across Bear Creek where he would be poised with head held down and slightly to one side, eyes fixed on the approaching enemies. When the two Labs were about ten feet from the creek, he would spring into action. Lad had developed what I called his drowning methodology. In less than a minute he had both huge black dogs on their backs in the creek and was angrily trying to drown them in the one foot deep water. He never killed them, but I'm sure he established a definite line that they were not ever to cross.

Every week-end during her freshman year in college, Spring would come home. Many times in the dead of winter we would all walk Lad late at night on those cold, snowy winter evenings. Ice would develop in November and usually stay on our streets until February. The four of us and the dog would literally skate through the storm for blocks as Lad got his nightly visit to the fields surrounding our house. He shared this ritual with us as we all renewed the family ties in times that were a-changing. Once again, the dog became the focus of our family activity.

On a night in 1976 when Lad was fourteen years old, Summer and I were watching television as the great dog lay sleeping on the floor near us. Sage was away at college, Spring had been married and was living in Texas, and things were much quieter in the Hawke household. Down on the floor Lad began to wheeze and choke as if trying to catch his breath, and Mitzie, his old nemesis, had come out and was sitting near his head in an obvious attempt to comfort him. Summer and I knew immediately that something was desperately wrong. It was ten at night, and we were unable to rouse our regular vet. We called a vet about four miles north of town, and he agreed to meet us at his office. The trip to his office was awful, but worse things lay ahead. He quickly examined our old friend and said, "His lungs are full of cancer. You must put him down."

Tears streaming down our faces, we carried the big dog into a concrete cell where the fatal shot was administered. We knew that the final sad act in this story was to call Sage, and tell him that the great dog's life was over.

37. TAKE ME OUT TO THE BALL GAME

My Uncle Aub bought me a crystal radio set kit in l945, and helped me put it together. We wired the antenna to my bed springs, and most times I could get, faintly, a radio station in Brooklyn, New York. This began my lifetime devotion to the professional baseball Dodgers, a team an earlier author had called the "boys of summer." My old bulldog, Kayo, and I spent dozens of summer nights listening to the exploits of Jackie Robinson, Gil Hodges, Roy Campanella, Don Newcombe, Pee Wee Reese, Duke Snider, Carl Furillo, Preacher Roe and company.

For more than fifty years now, I have lived and died with the exploits of the Bums. The list of great ballplayers, Hall of Famers, and real characters that that franchise has produced is unique in baseball. A few years ago, Don Newcombe, the Dodger's great pitcher of the late forties and early fifties came to Windy Gap High School to speak to our student body on the evils of alcohol and drugs. Big Newk has an official position with the present day Dodger organization where he works with their young players on those problems. He was a very effective speaker, and kept the high school audience spell-bound. Later, I got to spend a couple of hours talking with him about the "good old days". This conversation was certainly one of the high lights in my long relationship with the Dodgers. Newk was happy to talk with someone who remembered those exploits of more than forty years ago, and I re-lived those many golden days and happy experiences which I had spent as a boy following this great team. But time always marches on.

Now I am involved with my grandson Mark and the exploits of the new baseball franchise in our state, the Colorado Rockies. There are new baseball heroes now, - Andres Galarraga, Dante Bichette, Don Baylor, Pop Eye Zimmer, Larry Walker, Billy Swift, Joe Girardi, and Charlie Hayes. Last summer Mark came for a three week visit week with Grandma Summer and I. Naturally, we had to go to a ball game in Denver. The three of us rode a bus down to the stadium and climbed the ramps to the top rows of Mile High stadium. We seemed to be miles from the field. Seats for Rockies games are extremely difficult to get. These seats against the top of the stadium were the best that I could do six weeks before the scheduled game. That day there were 72,000 in attendance, and the Rockies were going to be playing the visiting Los Angeles Dodgers. I was in heaven (our seats certainly added to this perception as we were right up against the clouds). I was at a major league ball game with my beautiful Summer, and my grandson Mark, and my two favorite teams were going to play. What more could old Rock ever desire?

The Dodgers scored first and often. We watched the power hitting of the new Dodger sensation, catcher Mike Piazza, and the incredible fielding plays of Rockie first baseman Andres Galarraga. Mark got a great deal of enjoyment in watching the tough Rockie manager, Don Baylor, yank pitcher after pitcher. My grandson and I made many trips to the concessions area, and all three of us probably sampled every delicacy that the stadium offered. By the eighth inning, the Dodgers held a seven run lead and had their all star closer ready to pitch the ninth. I suggested to Summer and Mark that we start to make our way back toward the buses so as to beat the crowd. Certainly the Rockies couldn't overcome that much adversity.

Just as we finally cleared the main gate, we heard a great roar erupt from the crowd in the stadium. The Rockies were rallying in the bottom of the ninth. We tried to get back in to witness this miracle, but once you've left, you're out. So the best that we could do was catch a glimpse of the score board from behind the stands. The roaring went on and on, and the Rockies scored eight runs in the bottom of the ninth and won the game. Summer and Mark were completely disgusted with my decision to leave early, but all I could say was

321

that that kind of a rally in the bottom of the ninth was highly unusual. That was a pitiful explanation on my part as having watched major league baseball for forty years, I should have known that anything can happen and usually does. As Yogi Berra once said, "It ain't over, till it's over." I can hardly wait until the next time Summer, Mark, and I watch the improbable, and the magnificent. That's baseball.

38. COFFEE, TEA, OR VALIUM?

Summer and I have probably taken more than forty commercial flights around the United States. I would like to tell you about some of these trips which became adventures and/or misadventures. Our first flight took place when Summer and I were in our early forties. We flew from Denver to Houston with our son Sage to visit Spring and her husband, Chief, in their first apartment in Galveston, Texas. The plane was an old 747 with seating for ten across. We were seated in the middle section. It probably was a good thing that our seats were there, as I'm not sure we could have endured the flight if we had been able to gaze down at the plane's wings and the ground far below. Now I look back at my apprehensions on that first flight with total disdain, but our fears were very real than. I had flown in a small plane once before, but Summer and Sage had never been that far up in the air. We gripped our arm rests at take off, and gripped them again as we landed in Houston. The remainder of this trip was one of nervous anticipation, at least for me. On the way back to Colorado, we became seasoned travelers, even aware of the in-board heads and the availability of food and drink in the aisles.

In 1979, Summer, the Captain, and I made a flight down to Texas to see Spring. We were seated near the rear of the plane. Early on, Dad and I sat together, and Summer was right behind us next to an oil rigger who was flying back to work on an oil rig out in the Gulf. I had felt Summer tapping me on the shoulder for several minutes but thought that she was just being her affectionate self.

About thirty minutes into the flight, Summer was suddenly in the aisle looking down at Dad and I. "Don't you want to change seats with me?, she asked. I looked up stupidly, and didn't understand why she had asked the question. Then she said, "You <u>do</u> want to change seats with me." It seems that the rigger had gotten drunk as a skunk, and had been making moves on her. We exchanged seats, and I didn't know for a while whether or not I would have to stuff this obnoxious rough neck head first under his seat or simply slap him silly. He finally quieted down, and all of us settled back for the rest of the flight to Houston.

The very next year, we decided to fly down to see Spring once again. And once again, we decided to take my father along. It was during the time of a national airline strike, and we flew on an old plane staffed with a temporary crew. I looked very nervously at the battered condition of the plane's interior when we boarded, and my anxiety really increased once we were in the air. The wings of the plane were badly stained and vibrated violently throughout the flight. The total disintegration of the craft seemed imminent.

My dad, who always loved any kind of an adventure, stared eagerly at the flapping wings, and said, "This is great fun. I'm really enjoying it." The

Captain, my dad, had already began to suffer from the prostate trouble which eventually took his life, and on this particular trip, he had made several trips to the stainless steel mini-closet which passed for a restroom at the back of the plane. I saw the flight attendants begin the lunch service several rows ahead of us, and told Dad that he'd better go before we had the trays down and lunch was served.

"No, Son", he said, I'm all right. Five minutes after that we had a large tray of spagatti and fixin's delivered to our row, and he suddenly leaped up and said, "I have to go." He pushed rapidly past me toward the aisle, flipping a plate full of spagatti over my traveling clothes in the process.

It was also on this trip that we walked the Galveston beaches, played in the surf, and purchased the sea captain's hat for Dad. He wore it the rest of his life. We landed safely in Texas, but had to stop on the return flight for temporary repairs in Oklahoma City.

The following year, our granddaughter Jennifer was born. Summer had gone down a week before to help Spring with her new born, and the Captain and I flew down later to join them.

When we finally reached Galveston, I realized that I didn't know my daughter's address. So I had the driver drop us off in the area of town where I knew that Spring and her family lived, and the Captain and I walked with bags in hand until I recognized the right block and the right house. We were only six hours late, and all waiting for us were a little frantic.

One of my most eventful flights happened in 1989, once again the occasion was the birth of a grandchild. This time Michaela was born to our son Spike and his wife Pat. She was their first child, and once more again, Summer had gone down a week before I left to join them. My plane stopped in Dallas to pick up more passengers for New Orleans, but instead of de- planing at the terminal, the pilot taxied around the field for an hour before we pulled into a jet-way. Once there, the new passengers boarded quickly, and within a few minutes, the flight from Denver was nearly full. Then I all heard a disturbance near the front of the plane. Twenty Haitians had come on board, and there were seats for only twelve of them. The remaining eight refused to get off.

There appeared to be a language problem or misunderstanding of some sort, and no amount of explaining or insisting seemed to make any difference. The conversation just got louder and louder. It was a complete and total impasse.

Finally he pilot took off with eight people standing in the galley at the back of the cabin near the restrooms. It is the one and only time that I have ever seen a plane take off with people not strapped into their seats. The seat next to me had been empty on the first leg, but soon a huge woman was in it when the Caribbean folks came on board. She was immense. How she ever was able to get her backside into the narrow seat remains a mystery to me. But she did somehow squeeze in. It was on of those planes where the window seat is under the ledge of the overhead baggage area, and I was virtually smothered between this lady, the side of the plane, and the overhead ceiling.

About fifteen minutes after leaving Dallas, the stewardesses began serving a meal. The huge Haitian lady passed me a tray, and then tucked a napkin under my chin. I was mortified, but could do nothing but simmer. A few minutes later, she looked at me, evidently noticed some gravy on my beard, and took her napkin to reach over and clean my face. Holy shit! That huge black face with its startlingly white teeth wore a big smile, and I couldn't really be angry very long. We finally landed at New Orleans, and I made my way down the concourse to find Summer and Sage who had come to pick me up. No one believes this story even though I have told it far too many times. Coffee, Tea, or Valium?

39. GLITTER

Pictures of great wealth, complete depravity, great food, totally uninhibited actions, stories of the Mafia, magic, the brightest lights in the universe, and naked women made Las Vegas the sin capital of the world in my mind. I thought that an old prairie boy like myself would never indulge in this Devil's playground, but then it happened. In 1986 an old Wyoming cowboy, Bear Browning, and a prairie schooner, me, Rock Hawke, were sitting in the teacher's lounge after school one March afternoon talking about what would be an exciting spring break for ourselves and our wives. Bear asked if Summer and I had ever been to Las Vegas. That started our plans for an incredible experience.

The four of us flew out of Denver one night, and subsequently were deposited by taxi in front of the MGM Grand Hotel in Las Vegas at midnight. Ten thousand lights were on in front of the hotel. It was

330

brighter than high noon on the prairie. Even though it was the middle of the night, people were everywhere, and dressed as if they were going to a wedding. We walked through the glass and polished brass doors into a world that took our breath away. It looked like a god-damn Hollywood set. There was an incredible mile long desk for checking in, and twinkling, noisy machines in straight rows stretching out to the back forty.

We had purchased a hotel/flight package back in Windy Gap, and so went to the front desk armed with our admission tickets. The little fellow working there told us they were short of rooms, but that they would put us on the top floor. We rode the elevator twenty-one floors up, and that made Summer mighty nervous. We found the rooms assigned and stepped into the one for Summer and I. The first thing we saw a bathroom. It was bigger than our whole damned house, and had mirrors all over the walls. You could sit on the pot and see a hundred images of yourself in that awkward position stretching out to infinity. Next we looked at the bedroom. There was a huge round bed with pull drapes on the sides, and, believe it or not, the ceiling was covered with mirrors. From there you stepped down into a sitting room with TV and comfortable chairs and a connecting balcony which revealed the million lights on the Strip. Wow! We all were dying to see what the Browning's room looked like, so we went down a hallway covered with red wallpaper on which were hung dozens of pictures of Hollywood personalities.

When we entered the Browning's room, we were amazed again. In many ways their room was similar except that next to their bed was a big hot tub filled with bubbling water. Their bathroom was even more spectacular than ours, and it had what Bear and I thought were two porcelain foot-washers built in next to the stool. Later we learned that they were called bidets, and were a feminine device. After the careful inspection of our temporary bunkhouse, we could hardly wait to get outside on the Strip. We walked out the front doors of the Grand and across the street to the Imperial Palace. It was filled with the same colorful lights, noise and confusion as the MGM had been. It was now 1:30 a.m., and we were getting mighty hungry. We all sat in a booth hoping to get a cup of coffee. The waitress told us the special was a breakfast of steak and eggs for one buck cash. We couldn't pass that up, and soon a large steak, two eggs and a mountain of hash browns was delivered. After all of the things which had happened in the last two hours, we decided to go to bed and find out if all this had just been some kind of wild dream.

The next morning we awoke to discover that it, indeed, was real. Once again, we had a great breakfast, this time at one in the afternoon, and then the girls decided to go shopping at a nearby fancy mall, and Bear and I walked a half mile down the street to the Frontier Casino. When we entered the doors a dude came up, pumped our hands and took us back to his office. He said, "Well, I see that you cowboys are here for a good time. (Bear and I were wearing our best hats and our high-heeled cowboy boots.)

"At the Frontier, we like to take care of you fellows. Here is a rodeo belt buckle for each of you, ten dollars worth of free chips, and coupons for two free drinks and two free meals." Bear and I looked at each other and wondered if the little fellow had lost his mind. But we took the loot and went out in the casino to play. Our first stop was at the black jack table, and we turned that dealer every way but loose. We were both a hundred bucks ahead, and looking forward to breaking the place, when a guy called a pit boss came up and relieved our dealer, and brought on a young woman smartly dressed in half a red dress. She sure would have caught cold out on the prairie. This young lass dealt herself seven straight twenty-ones, and our pile was gone. We were too, next stop poker for Bear, and those intriguing machines for me. I put a few quarters in, and hundreds began bouncing out with a clatter into the tray at the bottom. My good luck continued, and soon I had a bucket full of quarters. At that moment Bear came back over and said "I made fifty bucks. We better get out of here before they change dealers again."

I didn't know that you cashed in your silver before leaving, so I followed him out the front door toting a forty-pound bucket of coins. It was a half mile down to the next casino, and I had had trouble walking in my boots on those concrete sidewalks anyway, so it was a real struggle to get down to the Dunes. Bear showed me the cashier's cage and I finally got rid of my load.

We met the girls for lunch, and they told us they had bought comfortable shoes, and had seem many dresses that sold for more than a new Ford. That night we went to the showroom to see the Smothers Brother and Mac Davis. We also had our picture taken by one of those girls who would get cold on the prairie. What a wonderful night. Well, our two days were up, and we had to fly back to Colorado. Reluctantly we left this paradise, but I'll always remember the fun we had with all those mirrors.

40. SARATOGA AND ENCAMPMENT

It was one of the strangest and most humorous evenings we ever spent in a bar. It happened in the little town of Saratoga, Wyoming, which lies on the north side of the Snowy Range Mountains. One can drive over Dead Man's Pass and down into the western slope valley of the North Platte river. The valley sits between two mountain ranges and is watered by both the North Platte and the Encampment Rivers. It is filled with beautiful hay meadows and stands of cottonwood and aspen. Saratoga and its sister town of Encampment, lie at opposite ends of an eighteen mile long valley that runs into the interstate highway on the east and Battle Mountain Pass on the West. It is a beautiful drive of 250 miles from Windy Gap. You go north to Fort Collins, and then across the Wyoming line past the little town of Tie Siding and into college town of Laramie. Leaving that city, once again you turn northwest toward Centennial, and then over an alpine pass into the Platte River valley.

A warm July night in Saratoga provided us with a n experience we would never forget. Summer and I had gone to Saratoga with two old friends to stay at the historic Saratoga Inn and relax, spending some time in their naturally heated pool, in their many fine art galleries, on their great golf course, and hoping to spend some time fishing the Platte. At night there is the added attraction of live music in the Inn's bar and dance hall.

On that July night, we had had a great meal of game hens in the dining room and had adjourned to the bar. The saloon, itself, is interesting. A large picture window on the north side revealed a rough-hewn porch swing on the Inn's portico. The scene was then framed by several huge Blue Spruce trees. The lodge also contains a varnished pine bar room of about 35 by 100 feet, and also a huge natural stone fireplace, several rough pine tables and chairs, and a small dance floor opposite the picture window. We found a table, and Summer and our friends, Nell Mellor and Harris Burton, and I were enjoying relaxing when the "band" for the night appeared.

The entertainment consisted of one man, Tom Bishop. He had recorded back-ground music, three guitars, and a keyboard, all of which he was equally proficient. These musical trappings allowed him to produce relatively pleasant music. His repertoire of songs was large, and the enthusiasm of the dancers on the small floor in front of Bishop that night made it a festive occasion. The first couple to hit the floor were highly stylized. He was a thin cowboy of thirty-five with a straw Stetson and new jeans. His partner was a lady fifteen years his senior dressed in a crisp squaw dress and strapped dancing shoes. Both of these folks had obviously spent a lot time on the open range in the Wyoming sunshine. Their faces were burnt the dark bronze which you see on ranch folks. They danced double-time to everything, up and back, and then around square corners. They executed elaborate hand motions which produced twirls and oblique movements. They drew the attention of the crowd and murmuring of appreciation for their accomplishments.

Next there were two middle-aged couples - us. Nell and Burt were smooth 1960's type dancers who obviously had perfected their routine to a point of ease and grace. Burt is a virile seventy, and Nell is a classic Nordic beauty fifteen years his junior. Unfortunately, I am a club-footed bear on the dance floor, but my long-suffering and very pretty blond wife, Summer, had enough ability and confidence top keep us from stumbling or galloping. We four danced through three tunes, and then headed back to our table for liquid refreshment and rest. The real fun was about to begin.

Then the third group took the floor. The prettiest of the three women in the group and her beau of the evening were the first entrants. He was a cleaned up, but now sweating, Wyoming cow-puncher. She was dressed in white boots, black tights, a white frilled smock ending in ruffles at her hips, and her ensemble was topped by a lot of curly hair, and a black derby hat with a large white eagle feather stuck in its top. Their pace was frantic and wild, punctuated with loud wahoos at opportune moments. We couldn't believe our eyes and watched fascinated as this pair cavorted.

This scene exploded into unbelievable chaos as another female, dressed just like the first, and her partner came onto the floor. The only difference in the image the second woman presented was that she was two and a half times as large as the first girl. Her dance routine mirrored the first couple's gyrations. Her partner was remarkable in his own way. He was a boy of twenty wearing a baseball cap, olive-colored fatigues, and high top red tennis shoes. His movements were the wildest and most uninhibited of all. He pirouetted in his high tops in great circles on the floor. Soon this highly picturesque couple was joined by a third member -

another female. She also was dressed like the other two women except her smock was bright red, and she had a long-stemmed white daisy growing out of the top of her derby. But it was her shape that guaranteed special attention from all of us on-lookers. She was less than five feet tall and must have weighed well over two hundred pounds. Her dancing style, in conjunction with the second couple, was incredible. She spun like a top with one hand held stylishly on top of her derby. She seemed to be totally unaware of the spectacle, which she was presenting. Her wa-hoos must have frightened the mule deer for miles around.

These five people were indefatigable. They gyrated and spun through everything the musician could produce. Tom Bishop, on the other hand, seemed to be totally non-plussed. He announced to the room between numbers that this whole business had so flustered him, he had forgotten his own name. In retrospect, I believe that this strange scene seemed to really inspire him, and his music got better and better.

Finally, I went to speak to this strange group and discovered that they were a mother, two daughters, her son, and their friends. I learned that they attended all the advertised dances in southwester Wyoming. The women cooed when I congratulated them, and the son pumped my hand.

Our evening came to a fitting conclusion when the musician, prompted by the crowd, played Mac Davis' "O Lord, it's hard to be humble," We all sang the familiar refrains, and then stumbled toward our beds.

One other story of this area of Wyoming needs to be told as well. In 1979 our family took an unforgettable trip to Saratoga which we later called the great caravan caper.

Three Ford vehicles and twelve people made an unforgettable journey from Windy Gap to Encampment, Wyoming, (Saratoga's nearby neighbor) for an extended family vacation. The vehicles involved included a pick-up, an old station wagon, and an ancient delivery van which was painted in the colors of the U.S. Post office. The people involved were Summer and I and my father, the Captain, our daughter Spring and her husband Guy, my half-sister Marilyn and her husband Buck Schiltz and their daughter Jeanne Beth, and their married son Lauren, and his wife Diane, and finally, their children, Brad and Brian. My sister Marilyn and her family lived in Omaha, Nebraska, and had come out west to visit. Summer and I decided that the very best we had to offer them was a trip over the pass to Lake Marie, high in the Wyoming Rockies, and then a continuing drive down into the western slope valley of the Encampment River

With Summer and my father and I in the pick up, Buck. Marilyn, Jeanne Beth, Lauren, Diane, Brad, and baby Brian in a van, and finally Spring and her husband Guy in the old mail box, we made the first one hundred and fifty miles without incident. We stopped at a truck stop west of Laramie, and had coffee and rolls, and turned west into the big sky area south of Centennial, Wyoming. This is one of Summer and my favorite vistas, as the valley floor is a beautiful high mountain meadow with frequent sightings of circling eagles, wild horses, range cattle, and plentiful pronghorn antelope. The sky seems to go on forever, and the distant mountain pass is clearly visible forty miles to the west.

I was leading the parade in our old pick up that I had named the Mule, and pulled off the narrow two lane highway so that everyone could share our concept of beauty. The Iowa folk piled out of their van, but seemed to be immediately distressed by the forever blowing wind of that area, and the clouds of deer flies which soon found Lauren and Diane's four year old Brad and their baby, Brian. So we moved quickly on. Wait till we get to the top of the pass, I thought.

About thirty minutes later we drove through the picturesque town of Centennial and started our climb up Dead Man's Pass. This area is certainly one of the most beautiful alpine drives on all of our continent. In addition to the beauty of the rocky ridges and blue mountains, there are thick forests of Ponderosa Pine, quaking Aspens, and millions of colorful wild flowers. Near the top of the pass, just at timberline, you come upon a series of beautiful, blue, very clear, and very cold, mountain lakes laying at the base of a great gray granite cliff. They are full of rainbow and golden trout, and are some of the best fishing lakes in the state.

The crowning jewel of this series of lakes is Marie, a huge expanse of crystal water that is fringed by tall green pines. In previous years Summer and I, and our children had picnicked, hiked and fished there countless times. All four of us were in agreement that it was the prettiest spot imaginable. On one memorable trip, we had climbed to the top of the mountain overlooking the lake, and had virtually lost our breath at the great beauty of the place. So it was with anticipation of Iowan wonder that I led the caravan into a parking area near the lake. Once again, the Iowa folks piled out of their van. I had anticipated ohs, and awes, but instead the Iowa folk just wanted to quickly get back into the safety of their wagon and away from the ever present mosquitoes and deer flies.

I guess that you can never anticipate what folks will like. So, we started down the west side of the pass toward Encampment. This drive is as spectacular as the east side of the pass with a great forest and many more very blue lakes, and then you drop suddenly into a high mountain hay meadow that runs on both sides of the North Platte River. From the bottom of the pass, it's about twenty miles of driving through the wild hay country until you reach the old frontier town of Encampment. This location had been the western slope meeting of the mountain men and Cheyenne Indians a hundred years ago. When I had last seen it ten years before, the old main street still stood in its original frontier glory with the very picturesque Cheyenne Saloon with its ancient boardwalks as the centerpiece of this great old town. This building had particularly delighted me as a boy. What an incredibly bad surprise to find this entire street burned to the ground a few years earlier. I had told them about the great saloon with its hundred foot bar, and its cribs for the dance hall girls built at the top of an ancient log stairway. Now it was all gone. There was just one old Rocky Mountain Canary grazing on the grass which had grown up on the ruined site. Yet one more major disappointment. I couldn't help but remember Thomas Wolfe's, <u>You can't Go Home Again</u>. I sure as hell couldn't go back again, and the folks that I was showing this enchanted place to seemed bored by the whole thing.

We did find the old fisherman's cabins that Summer and I had reserved still standing, but once there, the new owners of the cabins tried to tell us that we couldn't have the great cabin that would house the whole crew. It had been rented over our reservation. My sister lit into the proprietor. She is a formidable woman, and finally the seven Schiltzes, and Spring and Guy were in that massive old cabin. Summer, the Captain, and I stayed in a small cabin just across the way. Well, we were there. In the days that followed, we explored the old Encampment copper mill, and Dad and I took Buck and Lauren fishing on the Encampment river, and then up to Hogg Lake where we saw a dozen different mountain animals. Lauren and Guy also investigated the remains of the stage station at the top of Battle Mountain Pass to the west.

Summer, Marilyn, Diane and Jeanne Beth explored the town, made huge meals, and took care of Brad and Brian. At night the whole crowd played a card game called UNO brought west by the Schiltz family. We had a great time with this game, playing it on an old split log table in the big cabin, but Brad decided that the table was also a great place to turn loose his little wind up car right into the cards at the most critical moment in the game. The Captain hollered with mock frustration at these interruptions, and a great time was had by all.

One night the four young folks decided to go dancing at the Mangy Moose Saloon just across the street from our cabins. I saw a motorcycle gang come roaring up, and swagger into the saloon. Not wishing to have the kids in any trouble, I told Dad and Buck that we were going across the street and get the young couples out. I was afraid for the welfare of Spring and Guy and Lauren and Diane, but was secretly looking forward to something I hadn't been involved in years. A real saloon brawl appeared to be on the horizon. Just as Dad and I walked across the street toward the saloon, the four young folks came safely out the front door on their own. Once again, I was made aware that nothing would ever be the same again.

Finally, it was time to start back. Out in the big sky country once again, the Mule overheated and brought our caravan to a stop. However, I had little anxiety since Buck was an old truck driver, and Lauren was a Ford mechanic back in Omaha. Our experts, however, couldn't find the difficulty, so we limped back into Laramie.

We parked most of the family in a restaurant, and the Captain and I went to find a Ford garage. After about a four hour interruption, we all started back to Windy Gap. I never really was certain how the Iowans and Spring and Guy felt about this adventure, but for Summer, the Captain, and I, this had been an experience that revealed how old we were getting, and how much time had passed since Encampment's glory years. I hereby resolve not to talk about the past so much. Too little of it remains to convince the younger generations of what had once been a reality.

41. GRADUATION DAY

Our nuclear family has seven college degrees among us. We have seen and been a part of many other graduations, but the two proudest for Summer and I were the times that Spring and Sage received their degrees. My wife and I worked with the goal in mind of sending our two children to good four-year colleges all of our working lives. Many times that goal seemed impossible to reach, but with good luck, bright children, and God's grace, these goals were accomplished.

Spring entered the University of Northern Colorado in the fall of 1973. Her degree plan was to achieve a bachelor of arts in education with the goal of teaching in the public schools as her mother and father had done before her. On week-ends that first year, either Summer or I, usually Summer, would drive to Greeley to pick her up Friday afternoon, and then take her back to her dorm at UNC Sunday afternoon.

Spring had been an honor graduate at Windy Gap High School, and continued her excellent academic work at the college level. She was engaged to be married the summer after her freshman college year, but didn't allow that to be a distraction, and kept her nose in the books.

After her marriage in the summer of 1974, Spring moved to Galveston to live with her husband, and transferred to the University of Houston. This meant that she had a hundred mile trip daily, up and back on the Gulf Freeway, and through the layers of concrete underpasses on the south side of Houston in order to attend class. She did this for eight semesters, and then the grand day of her graduation finally arrived. She graduated Magna Cum Laude.

Summer and I flew to Houston for the occasion. The graduation that spring at this huge Texas University matched all the stories about Texas you have ever heard. It was the biggest damn ceremony

I ever saw. Thousands of graduates, along with their friends and relatives, crowded into the mammoth basket ball gymnasium. It was an extremely colorful and impressive extravaganza. Instead of diplomas being awarded to individuals, whole academic schools of graduates would flow across the stage together for diploma recognition, and to receive thunderous applause from the audience. Spring was only one of hundreds of education graduates to make the stampede across the stage that day.

Both her parents were extremely proud of her. Summer and I rejoiced in the fact that we had made it possible for our first born to receive a college education. That is not to fail to acknowledge the five years of hard work, and the dedicated persistence with which Spring had pursued her degree. At a point ten years before, we would have said that a college education was impossible for a child of ours, unless they had worked their way through, or had been lucky enough to get a four year scholarship. I had gone the work-your -way-through route myself, and certainly didn't want that for my children.

That evening, Spring and Guy, and Summer and I had a joyous dinner celebration. Spring was lucky enough to get a job teaching English at Galveston Middle School that next fall. She was to continue there until the birth of her daughter three years later. Now, more than twenty years down the pike, she is still teaching as a member of the faculty of Coconino Community College in Page, Arizona. Sages's route to a degree was somewhat different. He was an excellent student and football player at Windy Gap High School, and received a four year Boettcher scholarship to the college of his choice within the state of Colorado. He wanted a top academic school, and chose Colorado College in Colorado Springs for his undergraduate degree. He graduated Summa Cum Laude, and Phi Beta Kappa, from CC in 1980. Spring, and Sage's grandfather, the Captain, and of course, Summer and I, were in proud attendance, and once again, had a joyous celebration dinner at the Antler's Hotel where Sage had worked part time during his undergraduate days

Sage entered the University of Colorado School of Law the following fall. His record of academic excellence continued as he was chosen the outstanding first year law student after his first two semesters of attendance at CU. After two more years of hard graduate work, he was once more an honor graduate, this time as a Juris Doctor, in the spring of 1983. Once again we had a grand celebration. The Captain and Summer and I rejoiced that evening with Spike for his great accomplishment. Our son worked the following year as a law clerk for the Colorado Supreme Court, then he was a poverty lawyer working for the government for two years in Alamosa, Colorado, and in the fall of 1986 he went to work as a staff attorney for the Fifth Circuit Court of Appeals in New Orleans, Louisiana. Now, in 1995, he is a supervisor of staff attorneys for that federal court. What a pair of incredible accomplishments by our children. Naturally, Summer and I are extremely proud of them, and thankful that our children did, indeed, have the opportunity for a higher education, and that they, indeed, took full advantage of that opportunity.

42. YOU MAY KISS THE BRIDE

Two of the milestones in our family history were the marriages of Spring and Sage.

In 1974, our daughter Spring married Guy Randall in a backyard wedding at our home in Windy Gap. Spring had just turned nineteen, and her groom, Guy, was twenty-three. Our daughter was about to start her second year of college, and Guy was serving in the United States Coast Guard, based in Galveston, Texas. The date was set for August 24, l974. Summer and I had worked hard for months before hand in an attempt to make this ceremony as very special as possible. With the help of many other people, it turned out to be just exactly that. Summer spent months designing and constructing a wedding gown for Spring. She spent literally hundreds of hours sewing the details of the gown into place. She organized the wedding, hired a photographer, compiled a guest list of over one hundred, sent out the announcements, arranged for a Roman Catholic minister (Msgr. Hoffman, the University youth minister) to officiate, organized the reception and prepared the food and drinks for the guests. Summer, her sister Marilyn, and her good friend Nell set up and organized the reception. Summer's step-mother Effie and her aunt Marjorie prepared hundreds of finger sandwiches. I cut up many pounds of fresh fruit, and we stacked in gallons of punch.

My main contribution was that I repainted the outside of the house, and planted hundreds of flowers in an attempt to make our back yard appropriate for the ceremony. Our son Sage, and his girl friend, Dana, were a great help to all before, during, and after the festivities. On the day of the gala event, we were ready. The weather cooperated, and the day dawned bright and beautiful. We arranged chairs and tables in our bright green, be-flowered yard. Our small fruit trees were producing their first crop of apples, and our backyard wedding had taken on an almost magical appearance.

All the invited guests and more showed up. Spring and Guy had prepared their own vows, adding to the beauty of the ceremony. Spring was a very beautiful bride, and Guy was a handsome groom. Somehow I got my little girl down the stairs off our deck, and to an altar we had set in front of a beautiful bank of grape vines. The minister and the bride and groom went through the ceremony without a flaw in this beautiful setting, and everyone in attendance seemed to be thrilled with the nuptials. The reception held in our house and yard seemed to be a thundering success. The gift table overflowed with beautifully wrapped presents. The guests seemed to be very happy, and consumed great quantities of food and drink. When our reception was over, many of us adjourned to yet another reception in Guy's mother's back yard. Under a brightly striped canopy, the wedding participants and guests once again indulged themselves on good food and drink

against a background of live guitar and banjo. music.
Soon the newly married couple was ready for their get
away, and the beginning of honeymoon wedding trip
throughout the western states. Sage and his buddies
had painted appropriate slogans on Guy's little green
car, tied shoes and cans on the back, and filled the
interior of the automobile with dozens of brightly
colored balloons.

We all watched with cameras flashing as the car
disappeared down the street with occasional balloons
being released in its wake. We had pulled it off, and
the kids seemed very happy. Summer, Sage, Dana,
and I then went back to our home, and the clean up,
which was much less exciting than the preparation had
been, began in earnest.

Sage's weddings (that's right weddings - they
thought that they should do it at least twice) took place
in 1987. Their first ceremony was planned for May
twenty-first in Jean Lafitte National Park south of New

Orleans, a place where they had spent many happy hours during the time of their engagement. Sage had recently secured a job as a staff attorney on the Fifth Circuit Court in New Orleans, and Pat was completing her masters degree in public health at Tulane University. They had decided on a wedding with just friends in attendance, deep in the Louisiana swamp. It rained cats and dogs on the appointed day, so the ceremony ended up in a road house near the park, officiated by a justice of the peace, reception to follow at Pat's house in New Orleans. We were thrilled with their decision to marry, but sorry that we weren't invited, a sentiment that I'm certain was shared by Pat's parents, John and Ann Mead of Long Island, New York.

That problem was overcome on October 9th of that same year when the Meads put on a second wedding for the newly-weds at a Catholic cathedral in Manhasset, Long Island, reception to follow at a very historic and sophisticated inn on Long Island. This time the wedding was attended by many relatives of Pat's, and by Sage's parents, Summer and I. The wedding apparel was very formal, The bride's dress was gorgeous, the bridesmaids looked beautiful in their dresses, and Mike and his groomsmen very handsome in their tuxedos. The maid of honor was Pat's sister, Lynn Kress from Atlanta, and the best man was Sage's old friend, Roger Miller from Windy Gap. The old catholic church was an incredibly lovely site for the impressive ceremony. The reception that followed was top drawer.

The food, music and festivities were as complete, and as marvelous as any wedding we had ever seen before. We all danced for hours to a very good band, and shared in the traditional reception activities. We got to meet, and soon learned to like very much, Pat's parents and literally dozens of her friends and relatives. Sage and Pat began their second honeymoon with a night at the Plaza Hotel in New York City, and then had a trip through the beautiful fall colors of New England. It was a marvelous experience for all, and Summer and

I, two folks from the Colorado prairie, were overcome not only with the emotion and beauty of the event, but by our first trip to New York City. As we relaxed on the four hour flight home to Colorado, Summer and I held hands and remembered our own marriage in 1954. Now, our children had both taken that very great step in life, and we had all gone through yet two more of life's many wonderful passages.

43. LITHUANIAN JOHN AND HIS MOUNTAIN GIRL

Summer's sister, Marilyn, and her husband, John, have always been a large part of our lives. I first met Marilyn when I was dating Summer before our marriage. We went to formal dances in Denver occasionally, and would stop at Marilyn's apartment to change clothes. At that time Marilyn had just returned from teaching in Greece, and lived in Denver on Capital Hill. She was an artist, and our first home was graced by several of her paintings. I thought, on first meeting her, that she was one of the most sophisticated women I had ever seen.

About a year after Summer and I were married, Marilyn asked Summer to be her maid of honor at her wedding. Her intended, John, who had come from Iowa, had lost his best man as that gentleman was, at the last moment, unable to come to the sister's old

Claude M. Higgins, Jr.

family home in Craig, Colorado, for the wedding. I hadn't met John at that time, but he asked me to fill in for the absent best man. Summer and I packed up our new baby daughter and headed across the mountains for the ceremony.

It was at this occasion that I really began to learn something, not only about John and Marilyn, but about the sisters' home and family. Both these girls were country girls who had acquired quite a bit of polish since leaving their western slope beginnings. Nevertheless, they were both mountain girls at heart, a quality which made them both endearing to all the people they were to meet in later life.

It was a beautiful church wedding that the prairie boy, Rock Hawke, really didn't understand or appreciate at the time. I was overwhelmed with becoming a husband and father at twenty, and unfortunately, that was more chain than I could swim with. That wedding began my education in the finer things of polite society.

Over the next forty years our two families grew up together, and shared the happiness and sorrow that comes with living on this planet. John and Marilyn became, not only our best friends, but the support personnel when we needed it most. They went to our weddings and funerals, and we were there for them as well. Over the years we learned a lot about each other. The sisters were each other's confidants, and spent a considerable amount of time on the phone when we weren't together physically. John came from an immigrant family of Lithuanian heritage. He had played college football at Morningside College, and had then come West to seek his fortune. He had become a finish carpenter in the Denver area before he met Marilyn. He remained a union man for his entire work career, and became highly proficient at his job. Both of us men retired around 1990, but the sisters continued to work at their chosen field of education - now, however, on a part-time basis.

It is very difficult to condense a life-time relationship into a few paragraphs. We have shared interests in raising children (them four, us two), celebrating holidays, and participating in a variety of family ceremonies: picnicking and hiking, golf, casino gambling, small-time investing, and in just meeting survival demands in the America of the twentieth century. Above all else, we have learned to know and love each other. Marilyn is very much like my Summer. Both ladies are well-educated, sweet, compassionate, very alert, and very concerned citizens of our society. John is a little like me in that both of us are devoted to our family, but much less socially responsive than the women, and to a certain degree, more cynical and tough-minded. It has been a perfect fit for all of us.

Recently both John and I have become physically limited from a variety of health problems. This, too, has provided for an understanding that exceeds the comprehension of many of our other friends. It is very important for one to have someone in life whom you can count on, and someone who understands exactly where you are in time. Lithuatian John and his mountain girl, Marilyn, are those two people for Summer and for me.

Claude M. Higgins, Jr.

PART FIVE
CONCLUSIONS .

Claude M. Higgins, Jr.

46. THE CAPTAIN AND HIS LADY

My father and mother were products of their time. They had grown up during W W I, Cal Coolidge, Warren G. Harding, Prohibition, the depression, Franklin Roosevelt and the New Deal. All of these experiences shaped their lives for the next forty years, and to some extent, shaped mine as well. My Dad was a handsome, athletic, aggressive, fiery, twenty-four year old Irishman when he met my mother. She was just sixteen and in high school in Omaha, Nebraska. She evidently was mature for her age, always a beautiful woman, had a fiery temper, and played piano and sang on local radio when she wasn't in class. They had a whirlwind courtship that included many exciting nights of dancing at an Omaha tavern where they soon became the stars of the show. My mother was a dark-eyed beauty, and my father was kind of a cross between Errol Flynn and Humphrey Bogart. Physically, he most resembled Bogart. In character and personality, he was Flynn. It was an explosive combination. Both had dangerous tempers and very strong emotions.

There was a dark secret that hung over their union for forty-five years. It wasn't until my mother had been dead two years that I discovered that my father had been married earlier to another woman and that he had a daughter. His relationship with that first wife had gone bad and they were divorced. He evidently found my lovely, multi-talented mother to be just what he was looking for after his divorce.

For reasons Summer and I never understood, they kept the first marriage and the daughter, my half-sister, Marilyn, a secret from my mother's family and from me. Luckily, I found my half-sister when both of us were in our forties. Marilyn, her husband, Buck, her sons, Lauren and Rod, and her daughter Jeanne Beth, have been wonderful additions to the lives of the Hawke family.

When my mother and father were married, the time was 1934, and America was deep in the Great Depression. They picked a most awkward time in history, and in their own lives, to start a family. They were determined, however, to have what they wanted, and the marriage lasted until my mother's death, forty-two years later. I appeared eighteen months after my mother and father were married. As a boy, my father told me about his life-time adventures, but I noticed that he never said anything about the period between when at eighteen he had taught normal school, and then, at twenty-four, had been working in Omaha. I assumed he didn't say anything about this period because during this time he had been in prison. My father and mother set up a household in Omaha where Dad worked for a large department store chain as a department manager. Like most Americans of that period, my folks had a very hard time financially. I have heard many stories about trying to keep their family together on twenty-five dollars a week.

In l938, when I was three, my parents moved to Colorado where Dad had been transferred by the department store chain. We first lived a year in Greeley, Colorado, and then moved fifty miles east to Fort Darwin where at least parts of the family were to live for the next forty-five years. Dad left the department store business in 1939, and went to work for a Main Street shoe and boot shop in Darwin as manager. He continued this position until 1950 when my parents were able to buy the store he had managed for the previous eleven years. From that point on, mother worked by his side daily in an attempt to make their first real enterprise go. She had also become an exemplary homemaker and continued to do this double duty almost to the day of her death. Many people thought that she was the brains of the outfit, but I know that my father's charm also had a lot to do with their retail success.

My brother, Will, was born in 1942, and from that day forward (or so it seemed to me), he became the center of their lives. Both of my parents soon became regarded as mercantile leaders in Darwin. Both were also involved in the government and social life of our little prairie town. I felt that with all these activities outside the home, and with their concentration on Will at home, I was sort of forgotten. I spent as much time as possible with my Iowa grandparents, and with my aunt and uncle who lived in Cheyenne, Wyoming. By the time I was a junior in high school, I determined to leave home and join the navy. Luckily, the armed forces wouldn't have me, and I finished high school and started college at Colorado A&M in 1953.

It wasn't until I married Summer in late 1954, that they suddenly became aware of their older son. From that time on, I discovered how much they loved me, how much they really cared about what was going on in my life. That fact, along with the discovery of my life-long partner Summer, turned my life around. In 1955, Summer had our daughter, Spring. That irresistible little girl became extremely important to my folks, and to my bother, Will, who most unfortunately had developed a brain tumor at age fourteen, and was doing his damndest to battle the killer disease in his brain. Summer and I lived in a variety of rat holes in Windy Gap as I continued to work toward an undergraduate degree at the state university. I think that little Spring was a greatly needed point of relief for my parents as well as for Will, my brother, as he waged his losing fight against cancer. Spring became a symbol of young, healthy life in their world of impending disaster. The fact that our little daughter greatly resembled my mother was certainly another important factor in our very close family relationship.

Our second child, Sage, was born in 1958, and this bright, alert, little fellow also won all our hearts. I had graduated from the Colorado University with a degree in secondary education and a teacher's certificate in 1958, and our little family decided to pass up an assured job in Windy Gap, and move back to Fort Darwin where we could help my family during Will's last terrible years. Summer and our two little children stayed at my parent's house during the day-time taking care of Will six days a week, which allowed both my parents to continue to work. This was absolutely necessary for them as Will's many operations and hospitalization had drained all the family resources, and my parents had never carried health insurance of any kind. Our sacrifice probably helped them all tremendously, but it robbed my own little family of anything resembling a normal family existence. We spent all our free time with them. Summer and the kids were there all week, and then every Sunday afternoon, we went back over to their house for Sunday supper and an evening of television.

Will died in 1962, and Summer and I began to think about developing a career of our own and a home of our own somewhere else. Within a year, however, my mother, who had completely worn herself out during Will's ordeal, was diagnosed with terminal cancer as well. We were to spend yet another five years in Darwin trying very hard to help our family once again in their time of need. In 1967 my little family finally moved back to Windy Gap. Summer needed to finish her education, our family badly needed two teacher's salaries to survive, and our children really needed relief from the medical problems which had overwhelmed us all during the troubles of my brother and mother.

In 1976, my mother died. After her death, my father was totally lost. My mother had been the center of his existence. We went to Darwin, or Dad came to Windy Gap on a weekly basis. We included him in nearly all our family activities. Dad went with us on flights and car trips to see Spring (now married) and her family in Texas, and later to Arizona when Spring and her little family moved there. Spring had finished her undergraduate teaching degree in Texas, and taught first in a high school in Galveston,Texas, and later was to teach Navajo adults out of the community college in Page, Arizona.

Sage, meanwhile, was progressing through Colorado College and the C.U. Law school in pursuit of a degree in law. Dad went with Summer, Spring, and I went to Sage's graduation from Colorado College in 1980 and C.U. Law School in 1983.. In other words, my father had joined our small nuclear family in every way. He was a delightful companion on most occasions as he had a great sense of humor, and was totally uninhibited. We bought him a Coast Guard Captain's hat during one of our visits to Galveston to see Spring. He wore it everywhere for the rest of his life, and became the "Captain" that I referred to in the title of this piece.

Dad was diagnosed with prostate cancer in 1981. Like my mother and brother earlier, he fought the good fight. He died in 1985, and I suddenly felt as if the life I had known for fifty years was now completely changed. My parents had been far more important to me than I had ever admitted before. Many of the great loves in my life were forever gone. Thank God I still had Summer, Spring, Sage, and a herd of little Hawke grandchildren.

Isn't it amazing that you don't understand or appreciate your parents until they're gone and you're old? My parents were very special people. I am eternally sorry that I didn't fully realize that while they were still here, so that I could have told them how I really felt. I hope that, somehow, somewhere, they know it now.

47. DUST

In 1989 Summer's step-mother, Effie, died in Concordia, Kansas. Effie and Summer's father, Frank, had moved there several years before so that Frank, who had suffered a debilitating stroke and heart attack, could be placed in a nursing home that the family could afford. Concordia was also Effie's girlhood home where she still had siblings living who could give her the emotional and physical support, which she badly needed at that terrible time. Frank had passed away in 1983, and Effie lived the final years of her life in a little house on a hill in Concordia battling cancer until her own death six years later. It was a very sad end to the exciting and productive life which Summer's parents had led in Colorado.

Frank had grown up on a ranch in western Nebraska, graduated from the University of Nebraska at Lincoln, married Besse Cram, Summer's mother, and then began a long career of banking. Besse died when Summer was eight, and a year later, Frank married Effie. Frank ran banks in the roll of President and CEO in Western Colorado and Denver. He ended his professional career working in the Treasurer's office for the state Of Colorado. Effie was a nurse, having graduated with her degree from the University of Kansas. She held the position as the director of student nursing at St. Luke's Hospital in Denver for many years.

When they moved back to Kansas, we usually saw them only during an annual visit. I was always impressed with their intelligence, their happy and positive outlook, and their great social poise. We received the call telling us of Effie's death in the early spring of 1989. We jumped in our car and started the six hundred mile trek back to Concordia. Summer and I thought that we had really lucked-out on the weather, as that time of the year, horrible, blinding blizzards frequently blew through the country, but when we left

Windy Gap, it was clear and cold. As we drove through western Kansas, we noticed that many of the Kansas wheat farmers had done their spring plowing, and the land lay fresh and dark in the bright sunshine Things were about to change.

It was a very sad occasion as the family gathered, once again, to bury a parent. The day after the funeral we started back to Colorado early in the morning. There weretwo car loads of our family driving back that day. Summer and I left about an hour ahead of the other car. For the first sixty miles it remained clear and cold. The wind began to pick up near Salina, but we paid little attention to it. There was a little dust in the air, but the visibility remained reasonably good. Forty miles east of Salina, the wind was now blowing about fifty miles an hour. We could see great, five hundred foot high dust clouds building on the northern horizon. We stopped in Fort Hays for a cup of coffee and tried to decide whether or not to go on. We made a bad decision - we went on.

Ten miles later we were enveloped in an incredible dust storm. We literally could not see the side of the road or the front of the car. We dare not stop as we were certain there were other cars behind us on the concrete four lane, and they couldn't see either, and would certainly have plowed into the back of our car. We couldn't pull off as we couldn't see the shoulder of the road or the barrow pit, and had no idea whether or not we would be pulling into a deep ditch which would have rolled the car. . Almost totally blinded, we moved eastward at ten miles an hour praying that we didn't drive into something or that something wouldn't hit us from the rear. Long distance truckers were rolling by on the passing lane at about forty miles per hour. Evidently they thought, even though they couldn't see either, that no one would be in that lane.

Just outside of what we later discovered was the little town of Oakley, I nearly drove into a highway patrolman standing in the middle of the highway. He flagged us down and led us off the road into a barrow pit. I got out of the car and walked through that brown false night toward what seemed to be flashing red lights right in front of us.

One of those speeding truckers had slammed into the back of a white Buick, crushing it almost flat. There was a patrol car and an ambulance parked in the road. How they managed to get there, I will never know. A woman and her baby had been crushed to death in the collision. Emergency worker were trying to pry the flattened car off another victim who proved to be the dead woman's mother.

Sickened by the spectacle and unable to breathe in the great swirl of dust, I went back to our car. We had waited about an hour in that terrible brown cloud when we finally realized that the car pulled off behind us was the other Colorado car in our party. We were greatly relieved to find each other still alive, and struggled through the storm to say hello. About another hour later, the storm let up somewhat, and the highway patrol led us past the highway wreckage and off the highway into Oakley.

We all sought refuge in a truck stop, and had a greatly needed cup of coffee. We learned that there had been dozens of accidents ahead of us, and that at least fifteen people were dead. Summer's nephew said that we certainly couldn't go on, a decision we all quickly agreed with. He called around until he found us all rooms in a motel about five miles south of Oakley. Finally the storm had blown through, and we reached the sactuary of the motel without further incident.

On the next morning's drive back toward Colorado, we drove through the carnage of the previous afternoon. Smashed vehicles littered the roadway and lay broken in the ditches. We all said many thankful prayers for our salvation in the weeks after our drive through the dust storm. We had learned the real meaning of "dust to dust."

48. HOW HIGH THE MOON?

What kind of goals remain for Summer and I now that we have entered our sixth decade on the planet Earth? We taught a combined total of fifty-four years in the public schools, raised two children, have been further blessed with five grandchildren, and have worked at least a dozen other temporary occupations. We have put together a successful marriage for more than forty years, and have shared innumerable tragedies, and great moments of happiness. But as we enter our sixties, we often wonder, "What next?"

With my lifetime interest in literature, I have always dreamed of someday becoming a published writer, and thereby leaving something to posterity other than just increasingly vague memories of my sojourn here. Summer is service and people oriented, and is concerned with doing as much as she can to make the lives of others just a little better for as long as she has that opportunity. She has developed an interest in English as a second language, and volunteers at the university to help teach English to non English speaking adults, and to give them the tools to learn the rudiments of our language. Recently, she also has decided that she wants to leave a written record of family and life experiences. So here we are, two slightly past middle age people, many times just hammering away on our word processors.

We also both also feel the need to engage in activities with our life-long friends and relatives at every opportunity. Thereby, we schedule lunches, dinners, trips, etc., with these folks as schedules allow. We had planned on traveling a lot when we retired, but the side effects of my strokes and many surgeries have made it impossible for me to last very long on the road. We do try to make at least four week long trips a year, and usually several one or two night excursions. We spend as much time as possible in the mountains of Colorado and Wyoming, and engage in our life-time hobbies of photography writing, and sketching for Summer, and golf, fishing, and writing for me.

However, the question remains, how do we best spend our remaining time? Of course, our first priority remains to spend as much time as possible with each other, and as much time as possible with our progeny, but what else? Well, my goals are to write some really good stuff, and get published. I think that Summer would like to continue to teach, however that is possible. She has become a tutor for youngsters who are having either real or imagined troubles with their school experience., and is a volunteer instructor in adult ESL. I think that she would like to find a part-time teaching assignment that she could do regularly. I hope that both our goals are recognized before we totally run out of energy. But even if they aren't, I feel that we should continue to do what we are doing right now, and work to make the results better and better. If we improve on what we are presently involved in, perhaps opportunities will appear, and we must be ready to grab them if they surface. We also have to be conscious of getting ourselves in as good shape physically as is possible. Nothing will be possible unless we continue to maintain our present level of health, and hopefully, get progressively stronger.

When I look back over what we have accomplished in our first combined one hundred and twenty years, I am astonished and thankful, but human beings being what they are, as long as there is breath, we look for just one more adventure. How high the moon?

49. AND THE BAND PLAYED ON

I have two beliefs I want to share with you in this last section. I believe these things are true for all the members of the animal kingdom. I think they are most true for the leaders of our kingdom, us, man-un-kind.

In my life I have discovered that many times the end of something is also the beginning of something else. Our lives seem to be composed of cycles; we are either in an upward cycle or a downward, but at the end of each one, a new one invariably begins. The American Indian concept of the importance of the circle in life has a great deal of merit. We must always remember that there is some growth from destruction and death, and that the end of anything is really just the beginning of something else. Perhaps this is the basis of all religion. I know that it has always been true in my own life. There is great pain and grief in loss, but invariably, that is replaced with new challenges, new ideas, and new loves. This thought is many times little comfort in the midst of great loss, but it is a concept we must not forget. It is the sanctuary into which we retreat to escape insanity and desperation.

Secondly, we are all creatures of habit. As a species we seem to subscribe to the theory that an established routine is very important, and if one does something enough times, one will be able to find some great truth in that repetition. As I look at all the people and animals I know, it seems that they are relentlessly involved in the process of trying to prove this maxim. This behavior may either limit our accomplishments, or perhaps enhance them. God only knows. The comfort and security of the known is a powerful wall that separates us from the uncertainty of the unknown. There is also a human need to proceed toward perfectibility. This effort is impossible in any area in which we are unfamiliar. I believe that all humans strive to make even better those things which they deem to be the good things in their lives.

There now. I have that off my chest. No more philosophical stuff. Now there are a few more comments I want to specifically make about my own life. Second career commencement came for Summer and I in 1990 when we decided that fifty-four years of teaching public school kids was enough. We planned carefully for this great passage in life, but you are never really ready for that kind of a dramatic change. We weren't even ready for the small ceremonies which marked the end of arising at 6 a.m. and hustling to school through all kinds of weather (and there are some very unique kinds of weather here in the mountains of Colorado),and then buckling it on for eight hours of trying to communicate with, and control kids.

Change always requires adjustment. Our adjustment was doubled in that my health began to fail at the end of my teaching career, and many of the things Summer and I had talked about doing in retirement, suddenly weren't possible. But change also brings new opportunities and new perspectives. We have tried to seize both.

Naturally, we plan annual visits to both of our children and their families. We also make a couple of yearly visits to Nevada locations simply to unwind and enjoy the amenities of a luxury hotel. I am a dedicated life-time poker player, and Summer loves the shows and shopping that are available in Las Vegas, Reno, and Lake Tahoe. We try to visit friends in Colorado and Wyoming, and return annually to our old family vacation site of Saratoga, Wyoming. We both spend a lot of time writing on our computers, playing golf, fishing, and hiking. We have a monthly brunch with eight old friends, all of whom, with one exception, are retired educators. The men were all coaches, and the women share teaching careers, raising children, and loving grandchildren. This Brunch Bunch is an important support group for all involved. Summer and I also try to spend a good deal of time with my mother's sister, Elizabeth, who lives here in Windy Gap. We also like to visit my father's sister, Jean, who lives in a neat mobile home in Carson City, Nevada. Her housing location is an interesting one. She is only a few miles away from the Nevada attractions of Virginia City, the Mustang Ranch and Lake Tahoe. She is a fiery lady in her eighties who divides her time between being with her children, volunteering for the Catholic church, and holding on to her title as the best female slot player in the state.

In 1976, at the time of my grandmother's funeral, I made the amazing discovery that I had a sister whose existence I had never before known about. My parents and grandparents had hidden this relationship from me for forty-two years. During the time of my parent's marriage, one didn't talk about divorces, or half-siblings. Fearing that my half-sister might appear at my grandmother's funeral, my father broke down and told me the story. He felt that this revelation might make us disown him.

The only thing it did was to make me very sorry I had never known about my sister before. After a period of very tentative phone calls and letters, Summer made arrangements for us to go to Marilyn's home in Omaha, Nebraska, and for my sister and me to meet each other before it was too late. We hit it off immediately, and I suddenly had a sister, Marilyn, a brother-in-law, Buck, two fine nephews, Lauren and Rod, and a niece, Jeanne Beth. They are all good people. They have visited us in Colorado, and we have visited them in Nebraska. My two new nephews and my niece each are married with families of their own. In that moment of almost accidental revelation, I had acquired thirteen new relatives. Life is full of delightful surprises.

In this last section, I want to talk a little about my wife, Summer, and our more than forty years of romance. We began in a fever in 1953, and the fire ignited then has blazed ever since. Summer is a remarkable person who, in addition to being my wife, has been a crack public school teacher, and a wonderful mother and grandmother. She is also a remarkable woman. Intelligent, talented, beautiful, sensitive, compassionate, hard-working, and dedicated, She has lived sixty very productive years on earth. She is most generous, and always puts the needs of others before her own. She is not only my lover, she is my best friend. Nearly everything I have accomplished in life, I owe to her.

May God guard all the Hawkes and their loved ones now here, and all those to come.

Claude M. Higgins, Jr.

EPILOGUE

In August of 2001, the author of these stories, Claude M. Higgins, Jr., known to his family and friends as Mick, was found to have a brain tumor. As a result of the surgery to remove that tumor, Mick lost the use of both legs and his left arm. He fought hard to recover from many related medical crises in the five months that followed. During those difficult months, his courageous spirit and his warm personality continued to impress and inspire the many people involved in his care. As he left a nursing home to go to Craig Hospital in Englewood, the R.N. in charge of his case told him, "Mr. Higgins, you are the strongest man I have ever known."

At Craig Hospital, he received three months of intensive therapy. He delighted in encouraging the other people who were undergoing therapy with him. We enjoyed a lovely Christmas at Craig and were planning to bring him home when an infection spread throughout his body. Many specialists were called in, but the infection could not be stopped. Mick died in January of 2002.

Rock Hawke now soars over his prairie with the fierce wild birds he has always loved.

ABOUT THE AUTHOR

Claude M. Higgins, Jr., known to family and friends as "Mick", grew up in a small town in Eastern Colorado. He raised rabbits, roamed the prairie and listened carefully to the stories told by older men. As a teenager, he worked at many jobs and gave his teachers a hard time. He then worked his way through college earning an M.A, in English Literature. The crowning achievement of his 33 year teaching career was his development of a course in <u>The Bible as History and Literature</u>. He and his wife, Shirley, were married for 47 years. They have a daughter, Gayle and a son, C.Michael, and five grandchildren: Jennifer, Mark, Geoffrey, Michaela, and Kevin. His love of family, friends, teaching and animals shines through his writing. He was a vibrant, caring, unforgettable man.

49909706R00235

Made in the USA
San Bernardino, CA
07 June 2017